Mennyms Alone

Other Avon Camelot Books by
Sylvia Waugh

SYLVIA WAUGH was for twenty years a teacher of English literature. She always wanted to write, but *The Mennyms*, her first book, was not written until after her retirement. It was received with acclaim on both sides of the Atlantic. *Mennyms in the Wilderness* and *Mennyms Under Siege*, which followed, were received with equal enthusiasm. She lives in England with her husband and three grown children and is at work on the next book of this intriguing history.

Mennyms Alone

SYLVIA WAUGH

AN AVON  CAMELOT BOOK

AVON BOOKS, INC.
1350 Avenue of the Americas
New York, New York 10019

For my aunts, Grace and Elizabeth

Contents

PART ONE

PART TWO

Mennyms Alone

Part One

I have a journey, sir, shortly to go;
My master calls me, I must not say no.

—WILLIAM SHAKESPEARE
The Tragedy of King Lear

❦ 1 ❦

A Premonition

Sir Magnus Mennym lay listless in his bed in the best front bedroom on the second floor of the house at Number 5 Brocklehurst Grove. The window was open and sounds of distant traffic drifted in. It was a warm September morning, bright enough to make most folk feel cheerful. But Magnus was weighed down with a nameless misery. It had penetrated into the deepest fiber of his being. One purple foot dangled over the side of the bed. His white mustache drooped and his black button eyes had faded to a leaden gray.

Tulip came in and opened the curtains. She moved briskly round the room straightening this and tidying that. She knew only too well her husband's moods and she was sure that before long he would be telling her what he had on his mind.

Magnus's eyes followed Tulip's movements without any real interest in what she was doing.

"What are we?" he said at last in a voice slow and sonorous. "What are we?"

Tulip gave him a sharp, no-nonsense look.

"I don't know about you," she said. "I know exactly what I am. A wife, a mother, a grandmother and, suppose I say it myself, a very good businesswoman. Did

I tell you I'd written to New York? There's this shop called Bloomingdale's . . ."

Sir Magnus sat up straighter in his bed. His left foot touched the floor. He looked thoroughly annoyed.

"That is not what I mean," he snapped. "You know perfectly well what I mean. We are nothing but a family of rag dolls living for no other reason than that the spirit of Kate Penshaw could not rest easy in her grave."

Tulip sighed and sat down in the armchair by the bed. It would not be the first time she had lifted her husband out of a totally unnecessary fit of depression. It would probably not be the last.

"It does not matter why we are living," she said. "Just accept it. We are alive. We are lucky to be alive. And life is good to us."

"Not for much longer," said her husband. "Every day that passes brings us nearer to death. Did you think we were immortal?"

Tulip looked at him sharply, crystal eyes glittering. In the room across the landing, their granddaughter, Appleby, had lain lifeless for a whole year. In that time, Tulip had looked after her, kept her clean and neat and free from dust. The room had become a shrine and was a constant reminder to all of them that even rag dolls can die.

"The spirit left Appleby," said Tulip. "I am not so stupid as to think that it could not leave any one of us. But that is true of any living being, be it man, doll or dinosaur."

Magnus leaned forward, some vigor returning with the need to argue.

"Dinosaur is near the mark," he said. "We are about

to become extinct. That is what worries me. The death of any one of us, even Appleby, is nothing compared to that. If the spirit should leave me, quietly in the night, that would be no tragedy. What I am speaking of now is something different. I have a premonition, a dreadful premonition, that we are all about to die, all of us at one fell swoop."

Tulip looked shocked and angry as if her husband had uttered some blasphemy.

"What a dreadful thing to say! You shouldn't even think it."

"Send Soobie to me," said Magnus. "I must see Soobie. He will understand."

Tulip was surprised. Soobie, the only blue Mennym, blue from head to foot, was not usually a favored grandchild. Magnus regarded him with suspicion as one who was much too clever for his years. Soobie, like his twin Pilbeam, was doomed to perpetual adolescence. But not all adolescents are alike. Soobie's character was full of complexities. Old head on young shoulders, maybe, but with a heart forever innocent and caring. The rest of the family had all sorts of pretends to establish themselves as real people, but Soobie would never enter into them. He looked facts solidly in the face and was dogged in his acceptance.

"I'm not sure that seeing Soobie will improve matters," said Tulip. "The mood you're in, the two of you together could cast a gloom over the whole house. Just look what a lovely day it is. I'll open the curtains wider. Lie back and enjoy the sunshine."

"Fetch Soobie," said Magnus, grinding out the words, "and stop twittering on about the weather."

"It's the end of summer," Tulip persisted. "There won't be many more days like this for a long time."

"There may not be many more days at all," growled Magnus. "Do as you're told, will you? Go now and fetch Soobie."

The tone of her husband's voice warned Tulip not to argue. Without another word, she left him and went down the two flights of stairs to the lounge where she knew Soobie would be sitting at the bay window, watching the world outside.

The house where the Mennyms lived was not much different from the other houses in Brocklehurst Grove. Their neighbors were ordinary human beings, insofar as any human being can be described as ordinary. They never knew that Number 5 was home to an extraordinary family of life-sized rag dolls who had sprung into life after their maker, Kate Penshaw, breathed her last in a side ward at Castledean Infirmary. That was over forty-six years ago. The Mennyms, from seventy-year-old Sir Magnus down to the baby, Googles, had lived just like other people, but, unlike other people, they had never been any younger than their years, and they had never grown any older. Their origins had been a mystery to them for most of the time, but not one that they had ever questioned. Only in recent years had it become apparent that there was more to their lives than the trivial round and common task stretching on and on into eternity. For the first forty years of their existence they had thought that their life was permanent and that Number 5 Brocklehurst Grove was the safest place on earth.

* * *

Soobie sat down in Granny Tulip's armchair by the side of his grandfather's bed. His grandmother looked from one to another, hesitating, but then left the two closeted together like conspirators.

Soobie felt uncomfortable. He had been summoned to Granpa's room, he alone, and he did not know what to make of it. It was unusual. It was unheard of. Soobie was suspicious.

"You sent for me," he said abruptly.

"You're my grandson;" said Magnus. "If I wish to see you, I send for you."

They were like two fighters circling, each very wary of the other.

"So now I am here," said Soobie, "what is it that you want?"

Magnus sighed. To say what he wanted to say was not easy. The words nearly choked him.

"I want your opinion, your honest opinion."

Sobbie was astonished but irritated.

"In nearly half a century," he said, "you have never listened to any opinion of mine without pouring scorn on it. What value can *my* opinion have to anyone who is so bursting with pearls of wisdom?"

Magnus reached out his hand and laid it on Soobie's arm.

"I have never believed in giving you too high an idea of yourself," he said, "but deep down, you must know, I have always had a respect for your honesty and your sound intelligence."

Soobie looked him straight in the eye.

"There have been times in the past when I would have been glad to hear those words," he said. "I am

7

not sure that I care what you say about me now. What advice can I possibly give you?''

Magnus did not give a direct answer. He shifted on his pillows and said, ''I feel old, Soobie. Sometimes I feel older than the hills.''

Soobie suddenly saw his grandfather's agedness. His hostility melted and he was filled with pity. He *is* old, he thought, old and helpless.

''What do you want to know, Granpa?'' he said more gently. ''If I can help, I will.''

Magnus tightened his grip on Soobie's arm. Urgently he told him of the foreboding that had been troubling him for days.

''Something deep inside me says that our time is coming to an end. We are all going to die. I haven't invented it,'' he said. ''It is a real and powerful conviction. I don't know what to do about it.''

Soobie looked at him, searching, questioning. How true was it? How true could it be? Since Appleby's death, he had wondered about life on earth and when and how it might end. There had been one close call, but that had told him nothing. He could not envisage dying as something that could happen to him. To come close to death was one thing, to pass beyond it was incomprehensible.

What was he to say to his grandfather now?

Magnus waited in anxious silence. The clock on the wall ticked loudly.

''We did nearly all die last year, remember,'' said Soobie. ''Appleby almost destroyed us by opening the door in the attic. That could be what is preying on your mind. It preys on mine.''

"No!" said Magnus vigorously. "No! No! I wish I hadn't bothered to ask you. You are no use at all."

"I am sorry," said Soobie. "I really am. You asked for my opinion. I am just searching around for ideas. You would not want me to rush in with a half-baked theory. Maybe it *is* a genuine premonition. And if it is, it must have some purpose. If we had all died last year, without any warning, it would have been a terrible disaster."

"What disaster could be more terrible than all of us dying now?" said Magnus. "Our extinction would have been no worse then than now. Death is death."

"That death would have been total disorder. My hair caught fire. The blaze could have spread. The house might have burnt down. Father would have been found lifeless at work. The outside world would have asked question upon question, and never accepted any of the answers."

"That would surely apply at any time," his grandfather pointed out. "I will die in my bed, but there's no telling where the rest of you will be when it happens, or what you will each be doing. You all gad about too much for my liking. It could be a repeat performance."

"Not necessarily," said Soobie. "If we are all to die, a premonition could help. We could try to leave no trace of ever having lived. We could sever all contact with the outside world. If what you feel is really true, we might at least have time to prepare for an orderly end to things."

"So what do we do now?" asked Magnus as he considered these wider implications.

"We wait for stronger proof," said Soobie. "If your

intuition is correct, there are bound to be further signs. A vague premonition is no use to us. When we have a better idea of what it all means, then will be time enough to prepare."

"For that, we would need to know the day and the hour," said Magnus, clutching the counterpane with both gloved hands. "That knowledge is given to no man."

"But we are different," Soobie reminded him. "We are the creations of Kate Penshaw. Her day and her hour have been and are gone. It may be that *she* wants us to prepare. If she does, we shall need to be told at least the day if not the hour. We can't stop living and sit around idle for days or even months waiting for something that might never happen."

"So you do believe me?" said Magnus.

"I'm not sure," said Soobie. "It's not impossible. I can't say more than that."

❧ 2 ❧

They Don't Add Up

It was eight o'clock on a cold October evening. Albert Pond was sitting on the sofa in the Gladstones' front room, Lorna beside him, a mass of papers and old photographs scattered on their knees. It was a jumble of family memorabilia. There was a picture of Comus House, the gaunt place in the country where their great-great-grandparents had lived, and which Albert had eventually managed to sell. There was a picture of Number 5 Brocklehurst Grove, Aunt Kate's old home. There were papers about this, that, and everything.

Jennifer, Lorna's mother, smiled as they came across a thirty-year-old shopping list.

She was seated in the big armchair at the other side of the hearth, her feet tucked under her, enjoying the company of her elder daughter and her new son-in-law. In the background could be heard sounds of music and various other squeaks and creaks, not to mention bumps and bangs. This was the norm for Number 60 Elmtree Road.

Albert looked at the old black-and-white picture of Aunt Kate standing in front of the house in Brocklehurst Grove, a street a few miles away in neighboring Castledean. He felt a shiver run down his spine. To the best of his knowledge, he had never been inside this house. He knew Castledean quite well, of course. It was just the other side of the river from the smaller town of Rimstead where the Gladstones lived. He even knew that he must frequently have passed that very street, but that was all.

Yet it seemed to mean more to him than that. *And it did.* Two years ago, he had walked nervously up that very path and into the house. He had been accepted almost as a member of the family in the Mennym household, as if he too were a rag doll. But it had to end, and when it did, all knowledge of their existence was erased from his memory; otherwise, Albert could never have returned unscathed to his own world. It was a tiny miracle sent to put right the harm Kate Penshaw had done in calling on this hapless human being to rescue the Mennyms when their home was threatened with demolition.

Albert picked up some of the papers dealing with the will left by Chesney Loftus. He read through them.

"They don't add up," he said.

Jennifer looked puzzled. She saw that Albert was holding the Brocklehurst Grove papers in his hand.

"What do you mean?" she said. "It seems clear enough to me. According to Uncle Chesney's will, when the Mennyms die or move away, I become the owner of Number 5 Brocklehurst Grove. And, yes, I do see that that should be some time within the next few years. Even the son, Joshua, must be quite old by now. They were tenants for about forty-two years before Chesney died and, as far as I can make out, they were all living there in old Aunt Kate's time, before ever Chesney inherited.''

Albert smiled and pushed his hair back from his brow, a gesture his students were used to. It usually meant that he had something to explain and was diffident about explaining it. His mother-in-law, with her pale blue eyes and untidy fair hair, had the trusting look of a child. Albert himself was not worldly, but a certain scholarly logic made him suspicious of these Mennyms who were keeping Jennifer from what he felt was rightfully hers.

"This is what I mean," he said. "If you consider that Joshua was married with a fair-sized family forty-six years ago, he must be round about eighty now, if not older. That would make his father over a hundred, unless they all married at an absurdly young age.''

"I suppose you're right," said Jennifer. "I haven't really thought about it. I only knew about the will four years ago. All I remember of Uncle Chesney is Christmas cards from Australia when I was a child.''

"Let's think about the Mennyms," said Albert. "Are you satisfied that they are still alive?''

"Either Sir Magnus or his son Joshua is supposed to sign a declaration of residence each year on the first of October. A copy is always sent to me, as an interested party. Sir Magnus has not signed for the past two years," said Jennifer. "So I suppose he might have died. Or it could just be that the son was at home at the time and the father wasn't.''

"Sir Magnus might have died years ago," said Albert. "Joshua might be dead too.''

"He couldn't be," said Jennifer, still not grasping

what Albert meant. "His signature is on the declaration. It is the same signature as every year."

Lorna looked sharply from one to the other. She was more astute than either her mother or her husband, but Brocklehurst Grove was something she had never shown any curiosity about hitherto. It was just another family story, the sort her mother relished. At first it had given all the family a flutter of interest, but when it became apparent that nothing was going to happen there and then, they had dismissed it from their minds. The dictum *I'll believe it when it happens* was a popular saying in the Gladstone household. They applied it liberally to all promises that might or might not be fulfilled someday. Now, however, Lorna saw clearly what Albert was driving at.

Lorna and Albert had been married for just over two months. Besides being a distant cousin, Lorna had been one of Albert's students in her undergraduate days. After graduation she had taken a junior post in the university library. Her friendship with Albert had begun when she discovered that they were related. It had continued because they enjoyed one another's company.

One evening last winter, Lorna and Albert had been to a concert in Durham. Albert walked with her to the bus station.

"We're well matched, you know," said Lorna, her arm linked in Albert's.

"Yes," said Albert, without really taking in what she meant.

"Why don't we get married?"

Albert was startled.

"What do you mean?" he said, though what she meant was perfectly clear.

She swung round and stood still in front of him. The street lamps gave a fairy quality to her black hair and pale oval face. She looked up at him. The usual stray lock of soft brown hair flopped on Albert's broad brow. His thin face, high cheekboned, was also pale in the yellow lamplight.

"Will you marry me, Albert Pond?" said Lorna, her dark eyes twinkling. "It's not an idea I've just come up with. I've given it considerable thought."

"I'm too old for you," said Albert. "I'm ten years older than you are."

Lorna shook her head. There was a lot of bravado in her manner. Beneath it, she was nervous but determined not to show it.

"You couldn't be too old for anybody, Albert. You might be too *young* for me, but I think I can learn to put up with that. Give me a straight answer. Will you marry me?"

"Yes," said Albert, slightly dazed. "Yes. I will."

Lorna reminded him of another girl in another life. That the girl was Pilbeam, a beautiful rag doll, was something beyond recall. Only the feeling remained, the faint, forgotten memory of a true and pure love. But he knew that he loved Lorna, and he realized that she loved him. They were married the following year at the end of July, and set up home together in Albert's little house in Calder Park.

Lorna took the papers from Albert's hand and scrutinized them.

"I know what you mean," she said. "If any younger member of the family wants to go on living in Brocklehurst Grove they will not be able to do so once Sir Magnus and Joshua have died. That is very clear from the terms of the will. Chesney may not have intended to deprive you of your inheritance for very long. He would think that the family would have married and left home. The older generation might well have passed away or moved on by now."

Jennifer was mystified. She was far from stupid, but she was very innocent.

"Do you mean," she said, trying the idea for size, "that there is some sort of trick being played on us?"

"If younger members of the Mennym family are signing Joshua's name and he is no longer living there, that is not a trick, Mother," said Lorna. "It is a crime."

"That's putting it too strongly," Jennifer protested. "You can't go round calling people criminals even if you do have some sort of claim on their home."

"I can," said Lorna. "If those signatures are forgeries, then whoever signed has broken the law. Couldn't be plainer."

Jennifer looked worried.

"I am not going to accuse innocent people of doing something for which I haven't a shred of proof. It's not even as if I were Chesney's next-of-kin. It's pure luck that he decided to leave the house to me. Other members of the family have as much right to it as I have, maybe more. *They* are not complaining."

A door upstairs opened on squeaky hinges. The music became louder. In the hall someone dropped something and then cried "Ouch!" The noise was increasing.

Tom, Jennifer's husband and father of the whole noisy family, came in from the dining room.

"Has anybody seen my ruler?" he said.

"Never mind that," said his wife. "Come and hear what these two are saying."

Tom Gladstone was a primary school teacher. He had been in the dining room, preparing a chart for one of the next day's lessons. He stood and listened to what they had to say, talking one over the other.

"I don't see what you can do about it," he said. "It could be another ten years before your suspicions would be really strong. People are living longer and longer these days."

Albert said, "Well, Jennifer could always go round and ring their doorbell and introduce herself."

Jennifer looked aghast.

"I could not," she said. "I most certainly could not. What would they think of me? It would be downright rude."

"All right, Mum, all right," said Lorna. "Don't get your feathers ruffled. Nobody is going to make you do anything. Albert's just joking. But you have to admit it's intriguing. The possibility of fraud does exist—and if there is fraud, you are the loser by it."

"There is one other thing you could do," mused Albert. "You could write to these solicitors . . ." (he looked down at one of the papers) ". . . Cromarty, Varley and Thynne, and ask them to require Sir Magnus Mennym and his son Joshua to produce copies of their birth certificates."

"That's enough," said Jennifer shuffling the papers into their folders. "I thought Albert might be interested in our family history. I didn't expect it to turn into a full-scale investigation into people who are not part of the family at all."

"I don't see what harm there would be in asking for the birth certificates to be produced," said Tom, sympathizing with Albert.

"Well, *I'm* not going to write to the solicitors," said Jennifer. "You can if you like."

"I will," said Lorna, taking her mother's suggestion much more literally than she had intended. "I'll write a letter as soon as we get home tonight. I'll pop in with it tomorrow and you can sign it."

❧ 3 ❧

Appleby's Visitors

The family at Number 5 Brocklehurst Grove had no
idea that they were under suspicion. The declaration had
been signed punctually on the first day of October. Sir
Magnus Mennym's strange forebodings did not seem to
be linked to anything outside their home. They were all
aware of the shadow of Kate Penshaw somewhere in the
background of their lives. They all knew about the door
in the attic that must never be opened. If the end were
really coming, it would surely come by way of that door.
And it seemed to them that only the spirit who had given
them life could ever take it away. Magnus's premonition
was spoken of quietly by all the women of the house.
Encouraged by Tulip, they saw it as a reason to pity an
old man's folly. That was the easiest way of dealing with
it. To understand or come to terms with the reality of
death was much harder. So much they had learnt already.

Appleby was dead.

She was lying as if asleep on her bed in the back
bedroom. Her brushes were still on the dressing table,
her clothes still hung in the wardrobe. On the table
beside her bed a year-old magazine lay open at the
fashion page. The room was tidier than it would have
been had its occupant been living. Tulip kept it spotless.

The doll in the bed had red hair and green button eyes. It lay on its back with its arms out over the top cover. The hands were almost human with nails painted vivid red. But it was a doll. It was not the Appleby the family had known, the lively teenager who had driven them all to distraction with her maddening ways but had never once lost their love. And they still loved her. They loved the doll that had once been home to her spirit.

Pilbeam came in and talked to her.

"I miss you," she said, holding the lifeless hand. "Nothing is the same. I go to the shops and I imagine you there at my side, swinging along as if the street were your private property. I point to things in shop windows and say, 'Look, Appleby . . . ,' then I realize that you are not there. I miss everything about you, even your lies and your mischief. Will it ever be easier? Will it?"

Vinetta too would come to Appleby's room, late in the evening, bringing with her some sewing. She would sit quietly beside her daughter and remember. This did not happen every evening. It was no empty ritual, just a sober, quiet way of saying, I love you.

Wimpey, Vinetta's ten-year-old daughter, was the one whose visits were ritual. She had refused to believe that Appleby would never live again. Her mother had not had the heart to destroy this faith, but she channeled it into something gentle and harmless.

"You may look in on Appleby each morning," she said, after she herself had recovered from the shock of her daughter's death. "Don't go right into the room. Just open the door and say, 'Good morning, Appleby,' and if she replies you will know that she has woken up.''

It could, after all, come true. It could be seen as a prayer that might some day receive a favorable answer.

So every morning, without fail, Wimpey peeped into Appleby's room. At first she longed to hear her sister's voice, but as time went on she grew half-fearful that the doll in the bed would suddenly sit up and speak. She began to open the door the merest chink, to say "Good morning" very quickly, and to hurry away.

Tulip not only swept and dusted the room, she also brought in fresh vases of flowers. She brushed the red hair and stroked the doll's brow. Here for Tulip was a sort of peace. The others might fuss and quarrel. Appleby's quarrels were all ended. Granny Tulip was sixty-five years old, old enough to love the silence and the stillness of this one room in a busy, noisy house.

No other member of the household ever paid Appleby a visit. Wimpey's twin, Poopie, had his own way of not facing up to his sister's death. He never mentioned Appleby at all. He was not unique in this reaction. Joshua, Appleby's father, acted in the same way. When his daughter died he had been a tower of strength in Vinetta's time of weakness. As soon as a new normality was established he retreated into himself again. Months ago, Soobie had been taken by his grandmother to see Appleby "lying in state." Once was sufficient. He had stood at the foot of her bed and clenched his blue fists till the palms crumpled.

Oddest of all was Miss Quigley, the baby's nanny. Vinetta said to her one day, "Would you make me a portrait of my daughter?"

"Googles? Wimpey?" said Miss Quigley cautiously.

"Appleby," said Vinetta. Hortensia Quigley was a wonderful artist. It was in the January after Appleby's death. Vinetta feared, oh one cannot put into words what she feared, but because of her fears she wanted a permanent memory of Appleby lying serene and unblemished.

Hortensia said quickly, words almost run together, "No, Vinetta, I can't. Don't ask me why. I just can't. Her face is not clear in my mind, and I will never see her again."

"But . . ." began Vinetta.

"No," said Hortensia. "Don't ask. It's impossible. I prefer to remember her as she was."

No one in the household ever forgot how Appleby had died. Number 5 Brocklehurst Grove was not much different from every other house in the street, but inside the attic there was a door, a mysterious door that seemed to lead to another world. Wilfully disobeying Aunt Kate's command, Appleby had begun to open it. Then, realizing the danger just in time, she had put up a mighty struggle to close it again. Vinetta had rushed to her daughter's aid. Between them they had managed to shut the door, but at an enormous cost. . . .

Incredibly, heartbreakingly, *Appleby was dead.*

❧ 4 ❧

An Impertinent Request

The letter from Cromarty, Varley and Thynne was addressed to Joshua. It had not been an easy letter for the clerk to write because there had to be a vague way of asking for Sir Magnus Mennym's birth certificate while feeling uncertain whether the older gentleman was still alive. It would be much too bald and hurtful to say "if he is still living"!

". . . We have been requested by Mrs. Jennifer Gladstone to inspect the birth certificates of the signatories to the declaration of residence that you send to us on the first of October each year. As you may remember, Mrs. Gladstone has an interest in Number 5 Brocklehurst Grove. It may seem to you an unusual request, but if it is possible to comply we would advise you to do so. A refusal might lead to further action on Mrs. Gladstone's part and an effort to contest the will. This, we hasten to add, has not been mentioned. But it has always been a possibility, as with any will. We believe that it would be in the interest of all parties if the birth certificates could be produced . . ."

It was a very polite letter, topped and tailed with pleasantness. But it angered Sir Magnus, and it worried him. It worried him so much that he did not even take affront at being passed over for his son.

"They've got a confounded nerve!" he said. "How dare they ask for my birth certificate! Do they suspect me of some felony? A lot of sugary words and when all comes to all, they want to know how old I am, they want to find out if I'm still in the land of the living."

It was late evening. Tulip, Vinetta and Soobie were gathered round Magnus's bed, all considering what the letter might portend. Joshua had gone gratefully to work. Being nightwatchman at Sydenham's Warehouse might not be a very stimulating job, but it had its merits. It was so unsociable that no human being ever threatened his secrecy. And it was much more peaceful than staying at home. He could sit there in his little office, "smoking" his pipe and "drinking" cocoa from his Port Vale mug, while the others made whatever decisions they might want to make about the letter addressed to him.

Soobie was present because his grandfather had particularly asked him to be there. Since the premonition, Magnus had become increasingly dependent upon Soobie's view of things, regarding him as a sort of litmus test of reality in the world of pretends.

Tulip looked at the letter yet again, but no amount of looking would change the words on the stiff piece of paper with its flourishing embossed letterhead. Very official!

"It doesn't matter how impertinent you think this letter is, Magnus," said Tulip, "we'd need some sort of felony to produce a *birth* certificate for you. You have never had one."

"And even if we were capable of fabricating one," said Soobie, "it could lead to all sorts of other complications. We need time to think about it—months, not days.''

Magnus looked hopefully at Soobie.

"So what shall we do about answering this letter?" he said. "They've even sent a stamped addressed envelope for our reply. They clearly mean business."

It was not Soobie who answered him but Tulip.

"You must write a firm but polite reply," she said. Her gold-rimmed little glasses slipped down her nose and she looked at Magnus over the top of them. "Remind them that the will gives nobody any legal right to ascertain your age, and point out that the declaration of residence was signed just three weeks ago. Say that you will consider the request further when next year's declaration is due for signature."

Soobie looked satisfied.

"That gives us the best part of a year," he said. "We should surely be able to find a way round the problem before then."

Through his mind went the possibility of searching old drawers and boxes for a real birth certificate left by the Penshaw family, perhaps even Kate's own. Then there would be the business of forging copies with new details to fit Sir Magnus and Joshua, and of deciding on plausible dates of birth. Not the work of a day, or even a week. But given nearly a year, it might just be possible.

"What if they don't accept that answer?" said Vinetta, ever anxious. "What if they write again?"

"I don't think they will," said Soobie. "The law, as everyone knows, is happy to move slowly. But, just in case, I suppose we could add a pretend. We could say that the birth certificates would not be readily available. We could explain that the Mennyms came originally from Denmark and that the certificates would have to be obtained from the authorities in Copenhagen.''

It was quite a good pretend, a nice piece of embroidery. But Soobie suddenly thought of Appleby, weaving tangled webs. He was not happy with deception, even when it could make a useful contribution. Necessity is a dreadful taskmaster.

Sir Magnus had stopped listening. He would no doubt have approved the subterfuge, but his thoughts were elsewhere. The voices of the others had become blurred. A different voice was speaking inside his head.

Soobie noticed the unusual, vacant expression on his grandfather's face. The old man's jet black eyes had silvered over. His jaw had dropped, leaving a dark circle beneath his white mustache, a toothless doll's mouth made from velvet.

''Grandfather,'' said Soobie loudly and sharply. ''Do you agree?''

''Agree to what?'' said Magnus in confusion as Soobie's voice called him to attention. ''Agree to what?''

Patiently, Soobie explained everything again, even giving some idea of how the problem of birth certificates could be handled. Tulip was annoyed with her husband for appearing so stupid, and Vinetta was concerned. It was so unlike Magnus to lose the thread of the conversation.

Magnus, however, listened attentively now and gave his approval to the projected letter.

''You can write it, Tulip,'' he said. ''Let Joshua sign it. Now I would like a word with Soobie. Alone.''

Tulip pursed her lips and gave Soobie a disapproving look. What were they up to?

"Your grandfather needs his sleep," she said. "Don't stay here too long."

She looked at Magnus and added, "And don't you go filling his head with odd ideas. He has plenty of his own already."

Soobie and his grandfather were left alone once again.

"Come closer," said Magnus. "Sit in your grandmother's chair."

Soobie was puzzled but came forward obediently. Tulip's was a deep armchair on smooth-running castors. He pulled it forward close to the bed.

"Now," said Magnus, leaning toward him. "Listen to me."

"Yes?" said Soobie.

"There will be no birth certificates," he said vehemently. "There will be no forgeries. I know now that we have just one more year. That will give us ample time for all we need to do."

Soobie was silent.

"You know what I mean, don't you?" said Magnus, grasping his grandson's hand.

"I think so," said Soobie slowly.

"There has been a further sign, a speaking to my spirit," said Magnus, with a cautious look over Soobie's shoulder at the bedroom door. "October the first, next year. That is the day. To know the hour would be too much to expect. But for now, we must take our time. We must consider all that will need to be done."

Soobie shuddered, suddenly aware of the possibility

that Magnus might not be self-deluded. That spell of vagueness might not have been senility. In which case . . . ?

"You will have to tell the others," said Soobie. "It is not something we can keep to ourselves. Granny Tulip and Mother and Father should be told straightaway."

❧ 5 ❧

Telling Tulip

Next morning, when Tulip came in to open the curtains, Magnus said firmly, "Sit down, Tulip. I want to talk to you."

Telling Soobie had been no problem because Soobie was willing to listen. Telling Tulip would be a different matter. She had already rejected his first premonition.

Typically, she looked at the clock on the wall before taking her place in the armchair by the bed. She knew that Magnus was a scholar of some considerable reputation. His articles on the English civil war had appeared in all sorts of journals. But she had more to concern her than the everlasting Battle of Edgehill. Magnus could be very garrulous.

"It won't have to take long," she said. "I have a lot to do. It is the third Thursday, you know."

The third Thursday of every month was Tulip's regular day for attending to all the household bills. The ritual had begun in the days when they had paid rent to live at 5 Brocklehurst Grove. Their landlord, Chesney Loftus, lived in Australia. When he died he left the house to the Mennyms, not as an outright bequest but for "however long Sir Magnus and/or his son Joshua Mennym should continue to reside in the said property."

Tulip saw no reason for this new arrangement to change her routine. There was one less bill, that was all. It was a fairly substantial bill but certainly not the only one the Mennyms had to pay. Gas, electric, telephone, taxes, were all punctually paid and carefully recorded.

"It will take as long as it takes," said Magnus cryptically. He adjusted the pillows behind him to make himself more comfortable.

"Meaning?" said his wife warily.

"I have to make you understand what happened in this room last night," said Magnus. "You thought I'd dozed off, didn't you?"

Tulip was irritated. She had dismissed Magnus's lapse and was prepared to forget it. It seemed that Magnus was not. She was beginning to wish she had brought her knitting!

"Well, I didn't," said Magnus. "I went into some sort of trance, and while I was in that state I had another premonition, a clearer warning. On the first of October next year, the very day the signing is due, the spirit will leave us and we shall all die."

Tulip gave him a look of scorn.

"I have never heard such nonsense," she said. "You must have dreamt it! If you aren't careful you'll turn senile. Then what would happen to the Battle of Edgehill? Pull yourself together, Magnus. Don't be so foolish."

"I am the head of this household," said Magnus. He kept his tone moderate though he felt deeply insulted. "If I say I had a premonition, then I had a premonition."

Tulip looked impatient. She got up from the armchair and prepared to leave the room.

"I'm going now, before I say something I'll regret," she said. "I have neither the time nor the inclination to listen to fantasies."

She turned her back on him and walked toward the door.

Magnus raised his voice and called after her, "We *are* going to die, Tulip. We are all going to die. The day has been named. We must accept it, because we have no choice. And we must prepare, because that is our duty."

Tulip turned again, faltering. There was something so chilling in her husband's words. Was he going mad? Or mystical? Either possibility was unnerving. She sat down.

"Are you quite, quite sure you are not just imagining it? It seems a strange coincidence that the chosen day should just happen to be the day of the signing. That is how dreams work," she said, but in a much gentler voice.

"I know all that," said Magnus, putting out one hand to cover hers. "I can't help the coincidence. I can't explain it. But, I do assure you, I did have another premonition, a stronger one even than the first. It was the same as when Vinetta closed the attic door. Exactly the same. Why can't you believe me?"

He paused before adding in a petulant voice, "You believed Vinetta."

Tulip said nothing for a moment. Then she stood up again.

"I need to think," she said. "I'll go to the breakfast

room and do the accounts. It may become clearer to me as I work. Believing Vinetta was different. There was more evidence.''

Magnus saw how Tulip was struggling with the ideas he had presented to her. She would need time, goodness knows how much time she would need. She was such a neat, precise little woman with her white hair never out of place, her lace collars always just so and her blue-checked apron never other than stiff and clean. To accept something as fantastic as contact with the spirit of Kate would be hard for someone so conventional. She had no interest in contemplation. She did the accounts, managed all the family's money, and still found time to knit fashionwear to sell to Harrods. She was even talking about exporting her knitwear to America. Of all the Mennyms, she was the most earthbound.

Who was the least? Surprisingly, it was Joshua.

Magnus had less trouble in making Vinetta believe what had happened. She knew more about Kate than any of the others did. She had once known what it was like to *be* Kate. ''She was there inside my head,'' said Magnus to Vinetta. ''That is the only way I can describe it. It should have been terrifying, but because I was so much at one with her I could feel no fear.''

It was this account of his experience that made Vinetta give greater credence to his words than any premonition on its own would have done. And Vinetta in turn tried to convince Joshua.

''I suppose there could be some truth in it,'' said Joshua, sucking on his pipe. ''I wouldn't like to say. It seems to me, though, that we're in deep enough trouble over the birth certificate business without adding to our worries.''

They were sitting together at the kitchen table.

"Would dying worry you?" said Vinetta.

"No," said Joshua.

"Does it not make you sad to think of leaving this life behind?" She asked the question more for her own sake than his.

"No," said Joshua tersely. Then he relented and added, "I have worked my passage. When the voyage is over I shall not be sorry to go ashore, whenever and wherever that may be."

"But regrets?" said Vinetta. It was not that she wanted to cling to life, but she did love her family and she cared desperately what happened to them.

"No regrets," said Joshua. "Regrets are pointless. I can't know the future and I can't change the past. It *would* be good to go on watching the world. But then, who is to say that we won't?"

Vinetta shivered.

"That would not be my idea of Heaven," she said. "Just to watch and be able to do nothing? That could be terrible."

"Kate can't do this to us," said Hortensia to Vinetta as they sat in the lounge on the last day of October. Outside the rain was falling on dead leaves.

Hortensia accepted Sir Magnus's premonitions uncritically as terrifyingly, distressingly true. She took very seriously the threat of an end to living, to caring for Googles, to painting pictures and enjoying the comfort of her lovely room. It was heartbreaking. For most of her existence she had lived in the hall cupboard. *She* had not had forty-six years of this life, only five. That, she thought bitterly, was not long enough.

"If Kate's spirit leaves us," said Vinetta, "there will be reasons. It is not *our* place to question her decision. We are lucky to have lived so long."

Vinetta knew that there were other ways in which her family were lucky. Their death would be just a matter of having the power switched off, of their spirit departing into some mysterious hereafter. Illness they would not have to face. They could "cease upon the midnight with no pain," or at whatever hour Kate Penshaw should choose for her departure. The door in the attic would open and life in the house would end. Exactly how that would happen she didn't know; she didn't need to know.

By the beginning of November, all of the grown-ups, except Pilbeam, had had time to consider in some depth the premonitions. What they believed varied from one to another, and from day to day. Even Sir Magnus sometimes had doubts. In time, the first impact became blunted. It was an idea, it might come to something, but it might equally well fade away.

At Soobie's insistence, Pilbeam was not told. He did not want his twin to be troubled with thoughts of mortality. She, like Miss Quigley, had not had the same share of life as the rest of the family. For forty years she had lain unfinished in a trunk in the attic. Soobie had found her there. Vinetta had stitched her together and helped to bring her to life. Her living was a comparatively recent event. And in that short time she had both loved and lost. First Albert, then Appleby. It would not be fair to burden her unnecessarily with fear.

And if Sir Magnus were mistaken, if these premonitions were simply aberrations, then she would never need to know.

❧ 6 ❧

Jennifer

The letter from Cromarty, Varley and Thynne was couched in the most friendly terms. Their clerk was quite expert at sparing people's feelings. But Jennifer knew how to read between the lines.

She read it twice over, uninterrupted. Tom had gone off to work before the post arrived. Ian, the seventeen-year-old, had been stacking shelves in the supermarket for the past two hours. The younger children, Keith and Anna, were at school.

Only Robert, the eldest son, was still at home. He was studying for a physics degree at the local university. He came downstairs just after Jennifer had finished her second reading.

"You don't look too happy, Mum," he said. He'd followed her into the kitchen and perched himself on a stool. She filled the kettle for coffee.

"I'm annoyed," she said. "I'm vexed with myself mainly. Your sister . . ."

"Lorna again!" said Robert, knowing instantly which sister his mother meant. "What has she been doing this time?"

"That's not fair," said Jennifer, jumping to her daughter's defense. "She means well. She's just inclined to be bossy, and sometimes she bamboozles me into doing things I don't really want to do. She wrote to that solicitor and got me to sign the letter. Now I wish I hadn't.''

"Oh,'' said Robert, realizing what she meant, "the one about the birth certificates? Yes, I know all about that. I really didn't see much harm in it.''

"Well, I did,'' said his mother. "And I still do. More so than ever.''

She handed Robert the solicitor's letter.

"I don't know what you're so upset about,'' he said when he had read it. "It's a purely factual letter. The Mennyms have offered to supply birth certificates next year. They would find it difficult to obtain them straightaway because they'll need to send to Denmark for them. I don't know why that should upset you. The solicitor even says that he understands your concern.''

Jennifer looked exasperated.

"You do know what he's really saying, don't you? He's saying I had a cheek to ask. He is being very polite, but that's what he means. We should never have asked about the birth certificates in the first place. It amounts to harassment. It makes me seem like a vulture sitting on the fence waiting to peck their bones.''

"Mother!'' said Robert, laughing. "You do choose your words!''

"Forget it,'' said Jennifer, snatching the letter back from him. "You are totally insensitive. You haven't the faintest idea what I am talking about. It's no laughing matter to me.''

"I'm sorry,'' said Robert. "I do see what you mean, but you seem to be getting things out of proportion. I don't suppose the solicitor will give it another thought. And the Mennyms will probably forget all about it.''

After Robert eventually left for his morning lecture, Jennifer made a perfunctory effort to tidy up. Then she put some washing into the machine. But her activities were hampered by niggling thoughts about the letter. She heated some soup and grilled a couple of chops for Anna's lunch. I'll write the Mennyms a letter, she thought. I'll write and apologize. The chops began to sizzle rather loudly.

"I'm home, Mum," called Anna as she came in the back door. She was in her last year at the junior school. Next year, even she would be away all day. She sat down at the kitchen table to eat while her mother washed up the pots and pans.

"We're having our photos taken this afternoon, Mum," she said. "I'll have to put on a clean blouse."

The blouse she was wearing was still absolutely spotless. Anna was always immaculately dressed. Already, at eleven, she thought that grooming was very important.

Jennifer made no remark at all about the photographs. She was busy at the sink, washing out the grill pan. Anna looked up at her.

"You're not listening to me," she said. "Is something wrong?"

"Nothing," said Jennifer. "Nothing much."

Anna gave her a shrewd look.

"Is Lorna coming today?" she asked.

Jennifer flushed.

"I think so," she said. "It's her afternoon off and

Albert's down in Leeds for some sort of conference. She said she might come here after tea."

"I see," said Anna. She was very perceptive. When her mother was flustered it was usually because Lorna was being bossy about something.

At teatime, Anna was the first home. She feasted on scones, biscuits and a large glass of milk. After enquiring about dinner, she went up to her bedroom to do her homework. Keith arrived half an hour later, didn't bother with tea and went straight to his room.

Jennifer, peeling potatoes, looked anxiously at her watch. Four-thirty! She went on preparing the vegetables but listening intently for the next arrival. She was relieved to hear a car draw up and shortly afterward the key turned in the latch of the front door. It was Tom. Lorna always came to the back door and usually arrived on foot, having traveled by bus from Durham.

"Lorna's not here yet," were her first words as Tom came through to the kitchen. "I've had a letter from those solicitors. Read it and see what you think."

She checked the joint of ham that was roasting in the oven. Then she stopped to make Tom a cup of tea. He put the letter down on the table.

"Well, that's that," he said. "Looks to me as if you'll hear no more from *them.*"

"They must've been annoyed," said Jennifer. "They had every right to be. I'm thinking seriously about writing an apology."

"You can't do *that!*" said Tom, smiling up at her as she fussed with the plates. "It would only make things worse. Just leave it. If you don't bother any more, I don't think they will. I can't see anybody taking the trouble to send to Denmark for birth certificates unless we pester them.''

"Which we won't," said Jennifer. "We definitely won't. No matter what Lorna might say.''

She looked at Tom doubtfully.

"You try to explain to her," she said. "She never listens to me."

"Jennifer Gladstone," said her husband, "when will you learn to stand up for yourself? It's your letter and it's your decision. She can't make you do anything you don't want to do. What did your mother say?"

"I didn't ask her," said Jennifer. "I've never mentioned it. I'll be ringing her tonight, but I won't be saying anything about it. She's as bad as Lorna.''

"Yes?" said Lorna as she stepped in the door behind her mother's back. "Who's as bad as Lorna?"

Tom intervened.

"Your mother is upset about a letter she had today from the solicitor. You read it.''

He passed the letter across the table to his daughter.

"What a nerve!" she said when she had read it. "I don't believe a word of it. Birth certificates from Denmark! And it'll take a year to get them! They haven't heard the last of this!''

"Yes, they have," said Tom. "That is what your mother has decided. And it is her business first and foremost.''

Jennifer smiled apologetically at Lorna.

"Sit down," she said. "I'll make you a cup of tea. You will be staying for dinner, won't you?"

❧ 7 ❧

Pilbeam

"**W**hat are you doing?" asked Pilbeam. She had just come into the lounge, shaking raindrops from her long black hair and grasping her hands to warm them.

Soobie was sitting at the round table in the corner, not his usual spot, but a convenient place to write on a large sheet of paper. He gave a start and shuffled one paper on top of another.

"I thought you had gone out," he said, looking embarrassed.

"I went out," said Pilbeam, "but I came straight back in again. It came on to rain before I got to the end of the street. I hadn't taken my umbrella. So I changed my mind."

Soobie looked out of the little side window. It was raining very heavily by now, rivulets of water streaming down the glass pane. Not good weather for rag dolls, with or without an umbrella.

"There'll be no more going out today," said Soobie, thinking rapidly. "Let's have a game of chess. It's ages since we played."

He stood up and lifted the chessboard from its shelf, preparing to use it to cover his papers. But Pilbeam was not so easily sidetracked. She had asked a question and received no answer.

"What are you writing?" she said, moving the top sheet to reveal the one underneath. Pilbeam was very civilized, but she had never quite learnt how to respect her twin's right to privacy. Her black button eyes read swiftly down the list she was not meant to see.

"What on earth is that about?" she asked. "It looks like something Granny Tulip might write . . . solicitors, gas bills . . ."

Soobie snatched up the sheet. He was annoyed, but he said only, "It's a list of all of our contacts with the outside world, so far as I am able to make out."

"What would you want to know that for?" said Pilbeam. "You've missed out Bloomingdale's anyway. Granny had a letter from them just yesterday. And the Water Board. What's it all about?"

Soobie thought quickly.

"It's a simple precaution. You'll remember that those solicitors asked for Grandpa's and Father's birth certificates?"

"Yes," said Pilbeam. That was something she *had* been told. So far, Soobie had managed to stick to his resolve to tell her nothing of the premonitions.

"Well," said Soobie, "I looked carefully into the possibility of forging certificates. I even thought about using Miss Quigley's artistic talents, but it is really a non-starter. There is no way we could produce anything that would convince a solicitor."

"I could have told you *that*," said Pilbeam. "But you still haven't explained the list."

When Pilbeam really wanted an answer, she was like a dog with a bone.

Soobie persevered.

"My guess is that we will hear no more about the business. A year is a long time. It will be forgotten. If we are asked again, we'll just have to claim that copies are unobtainable. Pretending that they had to come from Denmark was quite a good ploy, I think. But if it comes to a real crisis, if the Gladstones insist upon knowing more about us, we may be forced to leave this house. And if we do, we will have to tie up all the loose ends."

Pilbeam gave him a fierce look. She interrupted whatever he was about to say next and asked sharply, "Where could we go? It's impossible, inconceivable. We can't have human help, we all know that now, and we certainly couldn't manage on our own. I'm not used to you telling lies, Soobie, but you are not telling me the full truth now. What does this list mean?"

She took the list from his fingers and looked at it again. Soobie gave a sigh. Pilbeam sat down at the table opposite him and waited for an answer.

"I didn't want to worry you," he said. "It's probably something about nothing. And these lists are just a sort of parlor game."

"But?" said Pilbeam.

Soobie saw nothing for it but to explain all about his grandfather's premonitions. Pilbeam listened in thoughtful silence. She recalled how withdrawn and subdued her grandfather had become. Letters out, once so important, were rare these days. He had taken the newspapers from her without even reading the headlines. She had put it down to grief for Appleby, but it would have to be a delayed grief. All summer he had been nearly cheerful, as if he had accepted his favorite granddaughter's death and was determined to go on living a normal, hopeful life. The change had come, she recollected, about two months ago. The change must have been brought on by these mysterious warnings prophesying doom.

"So," she said slowly when Soobie had finished, "if grandfather's vision is true, the spirit will leave us on the first day of October next year."

Soobie nodded, reluctant to say more.

"Then we shall all become as Appleby is now," said Pilbeam.

She looked thoughtful.

"Why did you not tell me?" she went on. "I had a right to know."

Outside the rain was falling even more heavily and lashing at the windows. The afternoon was growing darker. Pilbeam was sitting where she had sat that day, nearly two years ago, when Albert Pond had read a poem to her and she had longed for some magic to take her from her world safely into his. It was a bittersweet moment to remember.

Soobie, looking across at her, was visited with the same sad memory. So he answered quickly, "I chose not to tell you, deliberately chose not to tell you, because it seemed to me that you had known too little of life. Most of the time I don't believe in Granpa's premonitions. They are will-o'-the-wisps. Why should I trouble you with them? Why should I subject you to unnecessary fears?"

Pilbeam leaned forward and switched on the table lamp. In its circle of light the blue face, so serious, and the pale face, so serious, were clearly brother and sister, twin spirits, looking for meanings and fearful of what they might find. They sat in silence.

Then Pilbeam said, with a shiver, "I think I believe him."

"Sometimes, at twilight, on a gray autumn evening such as this, so do I," said Soobie in a voice as low as a whisper.

Suddenly the room was flooded with light. Granny Tulip stood in the doorway.

"Close the curtains," she said. "It looks as if it will rain all night. The daylight's just about gone."

Pilbeam obeyed her, still looking at Soobie.

"There is one thing we can do," he said. "We can try and make this the best year of our lives."

Tulip frowned. She said nothing, but she knew exactly what he meant. So he had told Pilbeam now, and this was the only consolation he could offer! Did he really believe in all that nonsense about premonitions? And whether he did or he didn't, why had he told Pilbeam? Or had she guessed? No one was quicker than Granny Tulip at reading between the lines.

❧ 8 ❧

Real Cake

At the end of November, Vinetta's thoughts turned to Christmas cake. Every year she mixed invisible ingredients in her largest earthenware bowl, whisking them round with a long wooden spoon. She always put in just the right amount of effort, as if the mix of flour, fruit and fat were really offering resistance. Then, when she was satisfied that she had stirred it thoroughly, she would tip the bowl and pour the make-believe mixture into a tin lined with real greaseproof paper. The cake went into the oven and was left to "cook" for at least two and a half hours before Vinetta carefully drew it out again, wearing her strong oven gloves, to check its progress. The oven, of course, was never really lit. A few days later, Vinetta would produce a well-dusted cardboard cake from the kitchen cupboard, place it on a real turntable, and mime to perfection the icing of it.

Every year so far, that was how it had been done.

Every year so far . . .

Every year till now!

This year Vinetta decided to make a real cake with real flour, real fruit, real butter and sugar, and half a dozen real fresh eggs. The recipe was there, handwritten, in an old cookery book that had belonged to Aunt Kate.

And the first thing to do was to acquire all of the ingredients, down to the last drop of almond essence.

With a headscarf pulled well over her brow, unbecoming but functional, and wearing her blue tinted spectacles, Vinetta went to Marco's, the town's largest, busiest supermarket where no one ever had time to look at anybody else. It is quite likely that had Vinetta gone there totally undisguised no one would have noticed her, but it is always better to err on the side of caution. That the currants she lifted from the shelf had been placed there that very morning by Jennifer Gladstone's son was just one of those bizarre unknowables that happen every day to someone somewhere.

It was ten-thirty by the kitchen clock when Vinetta reached home with her purchases. There was no one around but Wimpey, who followed her into the kitchen and waited to see what was in the shopping bag. Vinetta tipped the bag onto the kitchen table and set her purchases in order. Wimpey, standing by her, looked puzzled. She fingered the carton of cherries.

"What are you going to do, Mum?" she said. "People eat cherries, real people. We aren't people yet, are we?"

Wimpey cherished the idea that some day they might turn into real human beings, just as frogs become princes. Fairy tales are beautiful but very confusing.

Vinetta smiled down at Wimpey, her own little Goldilocks, golden curls tied in bunches with blue satin ribbon.

"We pretend things," she said. "But we do real things too. So this year I thought we could have a real cake."

"But," said Wimpey with her usual persistence, "what will we do with it?"

"We'll pretend to eat it, of course. What else? Now that's enough questions. If you are really good, you can sit here and watch me work."

Wimpey watched her mother put on her large work apron. Vinetta then took the box of matches from the mantelpiece, went to the cooker, opened the oven door and lit the gas. It was the first time she had done so since cooking a frozen turkey dinner for Albert Pond, two Christmases ago. Next she got out the scales to weigh the ingredients, paying very careful attention to the recipe book.

Wimpey had been sitting thinking.

"Can I ask just one more question?" she said. "Just a little one?"

Vinetta looked up from her work, her cloth face alive with the joy of working, flecked blue button eyes gleaming, gloved hands already powdered white with flour.

"Just one then," she said. "Then no more because I'll have to concentrate. It is not the same as pretending, or even remembering. It can go wrong if I'm not careful."

"It *is* going to be a real cake," began Wimpey. "So who'll eat it? I mean really eat it, after we've finished pretending?"

A sadness came over Vinetta, a shuddering sadness. She did not speak.

"Will Albert come and eat it?" asked Wimpey.

"No," said Vinetta wistfully. "No."

She gazed out of the window with a faraway look, suddenly drained of the joy she had felt just moments before. From the bare branches of a tree, winter birds were looking for comfort on a cold day.

"The robins can have it," she said, "and the sparrows. It can be their Christmas feast."

Wimpey said no more. Vinetta, determined to recapture her happy mood, set about mixing the cake. Some things she learnt for the first time. Creaming butter and sugar was much harder than she had ever imagined. Breaking the eggs one by one into the mixture, taking care to make sure they did not curdle, was great fun.

Wimpey would have loved to crack just one egg and let it slide out of its shell into the basin, but she hesitated to ask. Vinetta, usually so aware of what her children were thinking, and so ready to give in to their whims, was too engrossed to notice the look of longing on her daughter's face.

When the big bowl was filled with all the ingredients, Vinetta held it in the crook of her arm and vigorously stirred the mixture. She was surprised how difficult it was. It felt like churning cement. But she resisted the temptation to add more liquid. She was following the recipe to the letter and determined to do it exactly right.

At long last the mixture was ready to pour into the cake tin. Wimpey, large-eyed, watched every movement. Her mother noticed her at last.

"There's too much here for this tin," she said. "If you fetch the little one from the cupboard, you can line it with greaseproof paper and tip what's left over into it. Then it will be your very own cake."

Wimpey joyfully did as she was told and, with Vinetta guiding her, she held the earthenware bowl, gave a final stir to the remaining mixture, and poured it into the little tin. Then together they put their cakes into the hot oven and shut the door.

"Thank you, Mum," said Wimpey. "Oh, thank you!"

"Now you go and play while I wash up these dishes," said her mother. "We mustn't open the oven again for two and a half hours."

"What'll happen if we do?" asked Wimpey.

Vinetta had been born knowing the answer to that question. She smiled and said, "The cake will be spoilt. It will collapse in the middle and be good for nothing but pudding."

When the time was up and the oven door was opened, what disappointment for Wimpey! The big cake was perfect. The little one was burnt to a crisp.

"It's a beautiful shape," said Vinetta. "Just slightly overdone, that's all. My fault really. I should have known. A small cake takes much less time to cook."

Wimpey still looked disappointed. It didn't matter whose fault it was. It had been *her* cake.

"Poopie will laugh when he sees it," she said miserably. "They'll all laugh. Can I put it in the bin? Or don't tell them I made it. 'Cos I didn't really. You did."

Outside, a robin was perched on a branch. Inspiration!

"That robin looks hungry," said Vinetta. "I don't think he should have to wait till Christmas. As soon as your cake cools down, why don't you go out and feed him?"

And that seemed a very good idea.

❧ 9 ❧

A Real Tree

Every evening except Tuesday and Saturday Joshua went to work at Sydenham's Warehouse, walking the three miles there along ill-lit, quiet back streets. Summer or winter, he always wore a hood or a hat, and hid in his collar. He knew every step of the way, every curb and every cobblestone, and was constantly alert. There was one corner shop, for example, that opened late and displayed some of its wares on the pavement. It was a sort of general dealers, selling everything from postage stamps to potted plants. In autumn, roses ready for planting were arranged outside the open door. At other times, there would be seedlings in plastic cartons, bags of peat and boxes of bulbs. Joshua, head down and money ready, had bought one or two things for the garden at various times.

In the days leading up to Christmas, this year as every year, the shopkeeper placed real fir trees in barrels outside the window, tied loosely together with garden twine, three or four to a barrel, each individually priced. Other Christmases, Joshua had seen them and ignored them. The Mennyms had for a long time made do with an artificial tree which was brought out year after year, together with tinsel and colored baubles that had been replaced piecemeal as they broke or became too dirty to dust off. This year, in the week before the holiday, Joshua passed the shop on Sunday night, then again on Monday, and he paused very briefly to look more closely at the trees.

I'll buy one, he thought, on Sunday. On Monday his thoughts went a step further. I'll buy the biggest one.

Tuesday was Joshua's night off. He had come home from work as usual that morning and had slept till noon. When he got up he went out to the garden shed.

Poopie was there ahead of him, checking some hyacinth bulbs he had planted to bring into the house for the festival. Nothing unusual in that. It was something he did every year.

"What do you want, Dad?" he said, looking up from the bowls where fleshy greens shoots were showing nicely.

"There's an old tub somewhere over there," said Joshua pointing toward the darkest corner. "I've never used it before, but you'll know the one I mean."

The shed was lit by weak winter sunlight. In the dim area beyond the window were cobwebby shadows. Poopie got down off his stool and went to the far corner where there were things stored and never touched from one year till the next. He dragged out an old wooden tub, hooped with bands of rusty metal. It looked sturdy still, but very dirty.

"This what you mean?" said Poopie.

"That's the one," said his father, stretching both arms around it and lifting it up onto the bench.

"It's scruffy," said Poopie.

"It'll clean," said Joshua. "It'll be as good as new when we give it a coat of paint."

"What d'you want it for?" asked Poopie. It was after all, the middle of winter, not a time for active gardening.

"Wait and see," said Joshua. "We'll get it ready today. I'll be using it tomorrow."

Poopie, mystified, said no more but helped his father clean the dirt from the wooden panels and shift some of the rust from the metal. And when it came to painting Poopie took over completely.

"I'll do it better than you, Dad," he said. "I love painting."

"You'll have to put an overall on, and some garden gloves," said his father. "We can't go upsetting your mother."

Leaving Poopie to get on with the job, Joshua went to see Soobie.

"Going jogging tonight?" he asked.

"Probably," said Soobie grudgingly.

"I'd like to come with you," said Joshua.

"You don't jog," said Soobie. "You couldn't jog— not in the clothes you wear."

"True," said Joshua, not at all insulted. "A long topcoat is not much good for running in. Let me put it another way. When you go out this evening, I'd like you to come somewhere with me."

Soobie raised his eyebrows.

"I've some shopping to do," said Joshua.

Soobie had a growing distrust of the older generation. Granpa with his premonitions was more than enough. What was Father up to?

"What are you going for?" said Soobie.

"I'm going to buy a real Christmas tree," said Joshua. "They're outside the shop at the corner of Fulton Street. The one I want is big enough to hide behind. I'll take it inside. You can wait outside. But I could do with your help carrying it home. So how about it?"

"It must be nearly thirty years since we had a real tree," said Soobie, just vaguely remembering the pine needles on the carpet and Granny Tulip grumbling about them. "Granny won't like it."

"This year," said Joshua, "we are having a real tree."

He said no more.

They went out into the dark night to the shop on Fulton Street, walking together in silence, watching the ground at their feet, but aware of everyone and everything for yards around. There was not much to see, of course, but what there was, they saw.

When they were two doors away from the shop, Joshua turned to Soobie and said, "You wait here in the shadows. Keep your wits about you and be ready to run if need be." Then he hurried to the barrel that contained the tree he had already picked out for himself. It was still there, its price tag showing exactly what needed to be paid. Joshua had the right money ready. With a bit of a struggle, he tugged the tree from the bundle. Then he walked into the shop with it held upright in front of him.

"This one," he said, putting one gloved hand round the side of the tree to pass over the money. The shopkeeper checked the price tag and counted the coins.

"Need any potting fiber?" he asked as he peered hopefully through the prickly branches.

"No," said Joshua. He backed out of the shop and walked rapidly away. He and Soobie took turns in carrying the tree, one holding as the other helped to balance it and keep a careful watch on the road ahead. The street was empty. A fine drizzle and a cold breeze made the evening uninviting. The two Mennyms reached home safely and put the tree in the shed, ready to be potted next morning. Its tub had already been painted a deep holly green.

Everyone except Granpa came to the lounge to see the tree set up in the bay window. Vinetta produced a whole string of fairy lights she had bought at the market, together with fresh golden tinsel and exciting shiny baubles. Supervised by Granny Tulip, they all helped to dress the tree. In a final, ceremonial flourish, Joshua lifted Googles high in the air and Vinetta helped her to place a twinkling star on the very top branch.

In the days that followed, before the great day itself, parcel after parcel was placed beneath the tree. It would be a real Christmas, with a real tree, and gifts galore. . . .

❦ 10 ❧

A Real Christmas Day

The Christmas presents had all been opened, boxes and parcels and packages of all shapes and sizes. Their packaging was strewn all over the floor in the lounge. Vinetta was in the dining room, preparing the table for Christmas dinner. Joshua, in the kitchen, was taking refuge from the noise, wearing his new slippers and "smoking" his new pipe in the time-honored way.

In the lounge there was music. Well, a sort of music. Cacophony might aptly describe it. Poopie had been given a small electronic keyboard which he had set to play "Good King Wenceslas" over and over and over again. Pilbeam had bought Googles a drum, a very nice little drum with nursery-rhyme characters painted round the edge and a playing surface made of a tough sort of leather. Googles, in her high chair, wielded the drumstick enthusiastically. Wimpey had yet another new doll. It didn't talk. It was a genuine baby doll which when tilted would cry loudly and broken-heartedly as if it were starving, or at the very least had a nappy-pin sticking where a pin shouldn't stick.

Soobie, oblivious of it all, was in his usual seat, his ears protected by the headphones of his new stereo-cassette player. He had also been given a beautiful watch that told not only the time but the date. It could be worn underwater and had a battery guaranteed to last for three years! Pilbeam's presents were mostly wearable, and included a large box full of all sorts of makeup, most of which she would only pretend to use. The complexion of a rag doll does not benefit from the use of creams and lotions.

Granny Tulip came into the lounge carrying a big plastic bag.

"Now," she said very firmly, "you can stop all that noise for a minute and listen to me."

They all stopped, even Googles.

"Right," said Tulip. "That's better. You have more presents than ever this year and you've made more mess. Time to tidy up. We can't live in a shambles. Pilbeam, you can hold the bag. Poopie, Wimpey, gather up all those boxes and wrappings and put them in. Then, and only then, we will all go and have dinner."

At two o'clock precisely, they all sat down at the long dining table. Googles was in her high chair, between her mother and her nanny. The only member of the household not present was Sir Magnus. He had never gone down to dinner in all the years of his life. He could remember eating at the captain's table, long, long ago, but that was fiction. He could remember dining at his club in later years. But that was not fact.

The meal was surprisingly quiet and orderly. Joshua carved imaginary slices from the cardboard turkey, large thin slices that curved off the knife and had to be guided onto each plate. Vinetta poured invisible wine from a crystal decanter. The vegetable tureens were passed around, and the gravy boat. Then knives and forks were kept busy, emptying empty plates.

After dessert, they all returned to the lounge. Vinetta was determined to keep high spirits sufficiently in check to annoy no one. She sat in the middle of the settee, Poopie and Wimpey either side of her, and under her gaze the others took their places round the hearth. In the growing dusk of a dreary winter's afternoon, the family sat cosily singing carols. Table lamps were lit, the fairy lights twinkled on the tree. Had anyone in the street cared to look, they would have seen, indistinctly through heavy net curtains, the warmth of a family Christmas, the glow of festival.

After the Manger carol, they all listened sleepily and silently as Vinetta told the tale of the very first Christmas. Poopie sat, unchecked, with his feet on the settee and his knees up to his chin. Wimpey snuggled down under the arch of Vinetta's right arm. When the story was finished, she looked up into her mother's eyes.

"Is it a true story?" she asked, not for the first time.

And, not for the first time, Vinetta replied, "For all we know, it might be the only one."

They sang more carols, jolly ones full of merry gentlemen and bells ringing merrily on high. Then the curtains were drawn and the ceiling light lit.

"Now," said Vinetta, "for my surprise."

Wimpey smiled.

"Wimpey knows about it," said her mother, "but we have kept it our secret for weeks."

They all looked at her, interested.

"Just wait here for a few minutes and then we'll go back into the dining room."

When they got there, they found that the table had been laid again, but with cups and saucers and tea plates this time. They sat down.

Vinetta went to the sideboard and, with a slightly self-conscious flourish, brought her real, beautifully iced cake and placed it in the center of the table. After the "Oos!" and "Ahs!" were over, Pilbeam noticed that Soobie was not there. She was annoyed with him. Here was their mother doing something new and wonderful and he was not even there to see it. But before her annoyance deepened into anger, the door of the dining room was flung open.

In the doorway stood Soobie, and leaning on his shoulder was Granpa, looking magnificent. He was wearing a richly embroidered dressing gown, deepest emerald, reaching to midcalf. Underneath he had on not his usual nightshirt but a pair of shot-silk blue-gray pyjamas. His ensemble was completed with green velvet slippers and a silver-handled ebony walking stick. His appearance produced as many exclamations as Vinetta's cake.

Sir Magnus took his rightful place at the head of the table, causing everyone to move round.

"Now," said Vinetta when they were settled again, "I shall cut the cake."

Small rectangles of iced dark fruit cake were placed on every tea plate. The Mennyms fingered their teacups nervously and looked at the plates in front of them. Joshua took a sip of make-believe tea. Poopie copied. Then they looked uncomfortably at the cake again. Wimpey, of course, knew what should happen next, but she was a follower, not a leader.

"What do we do with it?" asked Poopie at last, giving his piece of cake a push with his finger. He had voiced the question they all wanted to ask.

Vinetta gave a severe look round the whole table.

"You pretend to eat it," she said. "You put it to your mouth and pretend to eat it. What else would you expect to do?"

Nothing happened.

Vinetta looked embarrassed. She was not willing to be the first to make a move.

Then Joshua slowly crumbled a piece of his cake, raised it to his lips and set it down again.

"I don't know when I've ever tasted a nicer cake," he said, smiling across at his wife.

The others, as if they had been given a cue they'd been waiting for, followed suit. Each piece of cake was crumbled and lifted and then nonchalantly returned to its plate. It made a change to pretend that the plates were empty, which was what they eventually had to do. Usually it was the other way round.

Sir Magnus had joined in reluctantly. He made a feeble, grudging effort at pretending. He broke the icing off the cake without allowing his mittened hands to make contact with the sticky fruit. He did not risk any crumbs reaching his long white mustache. Amid all the happy faces, his was the odd one out. One by one his family became conscious of his gloom. One by one they stopped speaking and eyed him doubtfully.

"I suppose," said Granpa, his voice cutting across the ensuing silence, "that you might as well make the most of things. This will be our last Christmas on this earth, our very last Christmas. *Carpe diem.* Seize the day!''

He looked so miserable that the thought of him seizing the day was incongruous. The others stared at him with varying degrees of understanding.

Poopie, leading as usual, braved his wrath.

"What do you mean, Granpa?" he said. "Christmas comes every year."

"Not for us, Poopie," said Magnus. "Not anymore. Fate has summoned us and there will be no turning back."

Why did he say that? Was his intent malicious? No matter what he really believed, he should have kept quiet. On this day of all days, he should have said nothing.

Tulip was furious.

"Stop that, Magnus," she said. "You are talking rubbish. You will frighten the children. Are you *trying* to spoil their Christmas?"

"Not one of you is too young to know the truth," said Granpa, glancing balefully round at all of them, even Googles who was nodding to sleep in her high chair. Miss Quigley put her arm protectively round the baby's shoulders. The old man at the head of the table, so lavishly dressed, had turned into a monster.

"Magnus! Magnus Mennym!" said Vinetta, moved to anger. "You are behaving like a foolish old man. Not one of us is *old* enough to accept your truth, your so-called truth. We have had a wonderful day and you seem bent upon ruining it. What's got into you?"

Magnus turned in his chair to face Vinetta. He was filled with rage.

"Don't you dare to talk to me like that! You all know that every word I have said is true. Think about it. Why have you made a real cake for the very first time? I'll tell you why—because you knew that it was your last chance. As far as we are concerned, there will never be another Christmas."

Then it was Joshua's turn.

"And what about that tree? It must be thirty years or more since we had a real tree. You knew, oh yes, you knew that this Christmas was special. Don't deny it."

Joshua didn't.

"You all know that the end is coming," Magnus said, flinging one arm out in a gesture that embraced the room. "Why else the extra presents, the special effort?"

No one said a word. Vinetta and Tulip were at one in thinking that silence was best. If they crossed him again, goodness knows what he might say. Least said, soonest . . .

Not good enough, NOT GOOD ENOUGH AT ALL. Magnus was aware that they were waiting for him to stop speaking, to let the uncomfortable truth slip away into silence.

"You are all doing things you will never have the chance to do again," he said insistently. "That is because you know in your heart of hearts that what I say is simple fact. Before another year is out, the spirit whereby we live will leave us, and we shall become what we really are—rag dolls, lifeless, useless rag dolls."

He banged his fist three times upon the table so that the cups and plates rattled. Crumbs of cake bounced off onto the tablecloth.

Wimpey jumped down from her chair and flung herself into her mother's arms, sobbing. Vinetta hugged her and said fiercely, "Your behavior is disgraceful, Magnus. Age is your only possible excuse."

Tulip stood up and resolutely took her husband by the arm. Then she turned to her eldest grandson, the one who might well be blamed for all this. Bringing Sir Magnus down from his room had clearly been a mistake.

"Come, Soobie," she said with ice in her voice. "Your grandfather is not himself. We must get him back to bed."

Magnus had had his say. He had given them something to think about. Now, exhausted, he allowed Tulip and Soobie to shuffle him away. The door closed behind them and those that were left in the room looked at one another anxiously.

"Did Granpa mean what he said?" asked Wimpey, still clinging to her mother and speaking in a trembling voice.

"No!" said Vinetta. "He doesn't know what he is talking about. He is very old. He has strange ideas. We'll take no notice of him."

"How old is he?" asked Wimpey, unsure of what *very old* might mean.

"Ninety," said Vinetta caustically. "When he behaves like that I feel he must be at least ninety, if not older."

But age had nothing to do with it. Age is often no more than an excuse. Sir Magnus Mennym had never been other than cantankerous, even in his fictional past. A middle-aged Magnus would have been a tyrant at work. A young Magnus would have been a spoilt, through glorious, brat.

❈ 11 ❈

Coming to Terms

"**I** have had no premonition," said Soobie. "This meeting is not really about anything as abstract or mystical as inner voices predicting death. We are at the beginning of a new year and before this year is out we will encounter problems that we have never had before. We don't need a premonition to tell us that. It is simple logic."

Soobie was sitting straddled across the high-backed chair in Granpa's room, his arms supporting his chin on the backrest. The expression on his face was intensely thoughtful.

The women were watching him, waiting for what he would say next. Sir Magnus looked from Tulip to Vinetta to Miss Quigley, then to Pilbeam. He felt a pang of jealousy as he realized that all four of them would give more weight to Soobie's words than to anything *he* might say.

The Christmas outburst had not been mentioned again, but the silence, the failure to argue, signified to Magnus a sort of disrespect. They were treating him as if he were an old fool, best ignored. Even this meeting, held in his own room, shades of past conferences, had been called not by him but by his grandson. Soobie had deliberately chosen an evening when Joshua would be at work. He knew how much his father hated conferences. He was also unwilling to have the issue clouded by an argument over when and whether Joshua should give up his job at Sydenham's.

"Well?" said Magnus sharply. "Get on with it. What is it you wanted to say? What problems has your superior intellect encountered? And what solutions do you offer?"

Soobie looked at Magnus, understanding his irritation.

"I have thought for months about your premonitions, Granpa. I have to be honest—I am no nearer believing you, or disbelieving you, than I was at first. But I do accept that there is danger. It seems to me that we have not paid sufficient attention to Jennifer Gladstone's request to see birth certificates."

"We don't need to," said Tulip emphatically. "We have resolved that one. We say that they are unobtainable and just leave it at that. That woman has no right to ask for them."

"You're missing the point," said Soobie. "Think of *why* she asked for them. She must be suspicious. She probably knows how long we have been tenants in this house. I've told you before. We don't add up. It is a problem that won't go away. The Gladstones, or some legal representative of theirs, will arrive on our doorstep someday, demanding to see either Granpa or Dad. Time has stood still for us. It does not stand still in the world outside."

Vinetta realized more quickly than the others what he meant. There could be a link between his logic and Magnus's mysticism.

"So Granpa's premonitions could be true?" she said. "I half-believed they were. It was so like my own experience of Kate."

"I don't believe," said Soobie, sticking rigidly to the truth as he saw it, "not in the way you mean. I have thought and thought, and I have reached what I hope is a logical conclusion. If we are really nearing the end of our time here, it seems very probable that Aunt Kate would want us to make preparations, like Noah building the ark."

"There can be no ark for us," said Pilbeam. "We can't exist without this house. We can't pack up our bags and go. Where would we go to?"

"That is why I believe that when the final danger comes, Kate will have to leave us," said Soobie. "She will have no other choice. Without her, we will cease to live, and it would be much better if we could do so in such a way that no one seeing us lifeless will suspect what we have been."

"That," said Magnus, rapping his cane on the floor at the side of his bed, "is precisely what I have said all along."

Tulip nudged her husband to be silent and removed the cane from his grip. Soobie was speaking and it was Soobie they all wanted to hear. He in turn gave an apologetic look at his grandfather before going on.

"If Kate wants us to have an orderly departure," he said, "it is perfectly obvious that she would have to give us a time. Otherwise we would leave loose threads all around. I am no mystic. Kate has never spoken to me or through me in any way that I can recognize. But, for the want of any other day or time, I am prepared to accept Granpa's word that the day will be October the first. In the months left to us, we must disentangle ourselves from the outside world. And when the time draws near, we will have to decide where we should be when Kate leaves us."

It was only then that the full horror of what might happen struck home.

The women looked shocked. It was possible to ignore Sir Magnus, but Soobie was a different matter altogether. He seemed to be presenting them with cold fact.

Vinetta squeezed Hortensia's hand, knowing how intensely her friend feared death. Tulip looked at her grandson aggressively.

"And what if you're wrong?" she said. "What if we make all sorts of preparations and the day passes just like any other day?"

"If I am wrong," said Soobie, "I shall look foolish, and so will Granpa. But would we mind? If we looked out of the window on the second of October and saw the dawn of another day, we would just go on living, and hoping that some other solution to our problems might be found."

Pilbeam gave her twin a long, searching look.

"That's not what you believe will happen?" she said.

"No," said Soobie, "it's not. That is why we must prepare. We have plenty of time. October is a long way off."

"What if Kate decides to leave us before this time that only Granpa knows?" said Pilbeam, suddenly realizing that anything was possible.

"I don't know," said Soobie wearily. "We can only

do our best with the little we do know. We are not in charge of the future. But then nobody is.''

''I have been as close to Kate as anyone could be,'' said Vinetta, adding her word. ''For a very short time, the whole of her spirit was in me. I believe that she really has told your grandfather the truth. Why should he lie? Why should she?''

Hortensia shuddered.

Tulip drew herself up sternly and said, ''I can see I'm outnumbered. All I can say is, I'll believe it when it happens.''

''You won't be here to believe it,'' said Magnus. ''You'll be as dead as the rest of us.''

''That is enough,'' said Vinetta. ''More than enough. We will go along with your prediction that the first of October will be the end of everything, but it is just January now. October is a long way off. We will not refer to it again till much, much nearer the time. And, especially, you will say nothing at all in front of the children. There is no need for them to know anything.''

12

Snow on the Moor

At the end of February, after weeks of dry, cold weather, it began to snow in real earnest. It snowed all day and all night, large flakes falling and lying. When Soobie looked out of the window early one morning, he saw the garden covered with a lumpy white blanket, shrubs and plants sleeping under a thick, thick quilt of snow.

Joshua came trudging up the drive in his stout gum boots, the hood of his old parka crisped with icy flakes. The journey from Sydenham's had taken him twice as long as usual. Soobie heard Vinetta greet him in the hall.

"There'll be no going out for any of you today," said Joshua as he removed his boots and shook his coat. "If I didn't have to go out in that, nothing would make me."

And the snow went on falling.

Poopie and Wimpey thought it was wonderful and wanted to get all wrapped up to go out. "Just in the back garden, just in the back garden. Please, please, please, Mum."

"If it stops," said Vinetta. "If it really stops. But I can't let you go out while it's still falling. Getting you both dry again would be terrible. It would go down your sleeves and everywhere."

She shuddered as she involuntarily remembered the time Appleby had been drenched right through. Memory is a joker, but the comedy is often black.

The young twins had to settle for watching from the window and waiting for the sky to turn winter blue. Brief interludes with fewer flakes flying raised their hopes, but they were dashed again when the storm came on as hard as ever. By four in the afternoon the snow was glittering under the street lamps and that, they both thought, would be that.

"Tomorrow, maybe," said Vinetta. "It will surely have stopped falling by then, and there is too much of it lying for it all to disappear overnight."

"It *has* stopped," said Poopie, his face flat against the windowpane. "It's completely stopped."

"But it's too late now," said Vinetta. "It's already dark."

Dark it was, but not late. Soobie looked at their disappointed faces and made up his mind to give them an adventure, an experience culled from his memory of times that never were. He went to look for Pilbeam, and found her listening to music in her room.

"I've had an idea," he said. "Let's take Poopie and Wimpey sledging on the moor."

Pilbeam looked doubtful.

"There'll be people there. Early evening, home from work. It could be quite busy with other folk having the same idea as you."

Soobie thought fast. It was a difficulty. He recognized that. But there was a way round it.

"We'll take them much later, when most children are

in bed. Then it will be quiet. We should have the place to ourselves.''

Pilbeam faltered.

Soobie said, ''Well, what about it? Shall we go?''

''Mother would never permit it,'' she said.

''She would,'' said Soobie, ''if we convince her that we can be trusted to take care. It could be our *last chance* of a real adventure.''

That was their winning card. Vinetta fussed but finally agreed. As quietly as possible, they went to the cloakroom and dragged out two large and ancient sledges, part of their inheritance, too big for the garden and never used by the Mennyms. Their metal runners were dull. Soobie greased them with a little rancid butter left over from the famous Christmas cake. Tulip was in the breakfast room. The conspirators sighed with relief when the preparations were over and the front door was furtively opened. Granny Tulip did not know a thing!

''Take care,'' said Vinetta in a whisper as she stood ready to close the door behind them, ''and don't be too long.''

Poopie and Wimpey sat one on each sledge, scarves crisscrossed over their hooded anoraks, their feet shod in wellingtons, their faces covered with animal masks, made of stiff plastic, that Vinetta had bought for them years ago. Poopie's was a tawny yellow lion's face with a flat brown snout and springy whiskers. Wimpey's mask was that of a misty blue kitten with gray whiskers and a little black button of a nose. Soobie had his hood pulled right over his brow with the drawstrings pulled tight. The rest of his face was almost completely hidden by goggles. Pilbeam was similarly attired but her hooded anorak was lined with thick gray fur.

They dragged the sledges along the snow onto the main road. Then, turning south toward Town Moor, they began to jog. Behind them, the younger twins sang "Jingle Bells." There wasn't a soul in sight. The snow on the Great North Road had been tossed to the side by snowplows lumbering through the darkness. A few cars passed at cautious speeds. None of their drivers took the slightest notice of the family party on the pavement, pulling their sledges over deep snow.

Before they reached their destination there was just one moment of fear. A police car stopped.

"Where're you off to this time of night?" said the policeman nearest them in a friendly voice. "You must be mad as hatters."

Pilbeam, taking her tone from his, said, "Yes, we are! We're having a midnight sledging party. Only it's not midnight, you know. Just half-past nine. We'll have these two home in bed well before the witching hour!"

The policeman looked down at the young ones, masked and hooded on their sledges.

"Mad as hatters," he said again, and the car drove away.

The police car was well out of sight before the Mennyms passed the three churches and the road that led down to the park. Then, looking carefully to left and right, they crossed the main road and went up the path that led onto the moor. The moon was not full, but the whiteness of the snow increased its light. On the horizon were two hills. That was their destination.

When they drew nearer, they found to their dismay

that they were not the only mad hatters in town. On the long southern slope of the hill to the left were about half a dozen skiers, some gliding down, others trudging back up. The hill to the right, shorter and steeper, seemed deserted. Soobie led the way to it. Poopie and Wimpey got off to walk. Then they all pulled the sledges to the top of the hill.

Fear again when they got there. On the other side of the hill, at its base, a group of revelers had lit a barbecue and were shouting and laughing and tossing snowballs.

"It's no use," said Pilbeam. "We'll have to go. If they see us, goodness knows what they might do."

"They're not interested in us," said Soobie. "They're enjoying themselves. I doubt if they can even see us. We can only see them because they have lights with them and they've made some sort of fire. And they're noisy."

So they decided to slide down the opposite slope, Soobie and Poopie on one sledge, Pilbeam and Wimpey on the other. Three times they went up and down. Then, on the third time, disaster! The revelers behind them had spread out. They had spotted the sledgers and they saw the chance of some fun. Snowballs came flying in their direction.

"Run," said Soobie to the younger ones. "Pilbeam and I will bring the sledges."

But running was the worst thing they could have done. The revelers were a rowdy bunch, happy to torment others. They chased after the family with the big old sledges. Snowballs caught them in the back and on the head. The way out seemed miles off. The Great

North Road with its tall orange lights looked like a mirage.

"Let's get 'em," shouted the leader of the following pack. "Let's grab their sledges."

"We can't outrun them all. I think we'll have to turn and fight," said Soobie, struggling for breath and too frantic to think straight.

Pilbeam was horrified.

"Oh, no, we won't. We can't. There is only one thing we can do—offer booty. Leave the sledges behind and keep running."

They did just that. Their pursuers pounced on the abandoned sledges and dragged them away, jeering and yelling like hooligans.

The Mennyms ran on, not even checking what was happening behind them. They came to the road and pelted across, not looking at all and just lucky that no vehicle was there to charge into them.

"That," said Soobie, once they were in the safety of their own quiet street, "is our last adventure."

Wimpey, bright as her own blue button eyes, looked at him sharply. She still remembered Granpa's words on Christmas Day. She still wondered what they might mean.

"Why last?" she said suspiciously.

Soobie took a grip on himself and said, "Well, we've lost the sledges for a start. And I wouldn't go through that again for anything."

❧ *13* ❧

A Quiet Spring

*T*he earth tilted and the snow ran away. Leaves popped back onto the trees, the sun winked and blinked in a changing sky, and then it was spring. The residents of Number 5 Brocklehurst Grove went on living their quiet lives and trying to forget Granpa's prognostications.

Except for Granpa, of course. He could not and would not dismiss them from his mind, and it was Tulip who had to bear the brunt of it. She was the one he saw most frequently, and she was the one he trusted least. Like Noah, he was willing to build his ark, but Tulip was a veritable Noah's wife, unable and unwilling to believe her husband's ominous predictions.

"Don't write back to those people in New York," Magnus said firmly. "There is no point in further complicating our life. It will be over soon enough."

Tulip glared at him but contented herself with saying, "Very well, very well. I'll file the letter for future use."

Then he told her to end her business arrangement with Harrods. And not to buy any more wool. And to simplify the family's finances so that their money could be disposed of in some suitable way before the final hour. And to . . .

"You're driving me mad, Magnus. I never come into

this room but you tell me to do something different,'' Tulip exploded one day. ''I do what you ask, even though I am not convinced of the need, but it is wearing me down.''

In the past forty-seven years, Tulip had, like the prudent servant in the parable, carefully invested the family's income so that it had become a sizable amount of money. She did not believe in burying their talents in the ground. When she perused the columns of the *Financial Times* it was pleasure and business combined. Forty-seven years is a very long time. Their wealth had accumulated, and only Tulip ever knew how much the family was worth. And it was part of her careful nature to ensure that fail-safe devices were in place to cope with her husband's demands that they should settle their affairs on earth. No step was taken that could not be retrieved when his wild imaginings proved to be just that.

Harrods was put on hold. Stocks and shares were sold, but the money was safely deposited in Building Society accounts where, when the time came, it would be possible to make ''contingency'' plans by depositing letters, to be opened only ''if the depositor should make no further transactions for a year and a day.'' The time stipulated was purely arbitrary. It had a nice legal ring to it! The letters, in any case, would never be opened. Tulip was sure of that. But, in the extremely unlikely event that Magnus's forecast should prove true, various charities would eventually reap the benefit. And each Building Society would believe that its eccentric depositors had left the country and had renounced all the riches of this world.

Confirmation of these arrangements would be sent to their own solicitors of many years, Rothwell and Ramshaw. The solicitors who had been involved in the administration of Chesney Loftus's estate were to be pushed into the background where Tulip felt they really belonged. Any hint of change was not to reach them unless it became inevitable. Tulip's system had so many cross-threads that it was bound to work. Come to think of it, it was not unworthy of a lady who had for so long been an expert at not only following, but creating knitting patterns!

The family deliberately avoided doing anything else that might be taken to be a ''last thing.'' Granpa's Christmas outburst had been a deterrent. The trip to Town Moor with its strong element of danger had been an awful warning. But, in the middle of April, Vinetta could not resist the temptation to do the one thing she had never dared to do. She went with Hortensia and Googles for a walk to the park.

For many years, Googles had had an old green pram which was taken no further than the back garden because Vinetta was terrified in case anyone should stop and admire the baby. When Miss Quigley took over as nanny, Googles was taken on regular outings because Miss Quigley had complete confidence in her ability to go unnoticed. The old pram had been replaced with a small modern pram, dull gray color, a sort of hooded carry-cot on wheels. It had the virtue of being very inconspicuous.

''Would you mind if I came along?'' Vinetta asked one fine afternoon as Hortensia was preparing to go out.

"I don't think anyone would notice, especially if you were pushing the pram."

Hortensia smiled down at Vinetta. The nanny was taller and slimmer than her friend and employer. One might almost call her gaunt.

"That's a splendid idea," she said. "It will do you good. And we'll see about who pushes the pram!"

They went along the street onto the main road, Hortensia pushing and very much in charge. Vinetta walked beside her, on the inside, with her right hand firmly gripping the handlebar. They turned down the steep hill that led to the park gates. When they reached the bottom Hortensia said, "Now it's your turn."

Self-consciously, Vinetta took over the pushing, both hands gripping the handle tightly. She looked, and felt, like a little girl taking out her new pram for the very first time. They went down the broad path to the lake. The park was quiet. The sun was shining but there was still a nip in the air—not quite summer yet. Both ladies were, naturally, wearing their glasses, their scarves and their gloves. Hortensia put the brake on the pram and they sat down on the park bench to enjoy the day.

"We should do this more often," said Vinetta. "I hadn't realized how quiet the park could be. And we have a very clear view of anyone approaching."

Hortensia said nothing. She was looking straight ahead, over the lake, taking in the sun glinting on the water, the trees on the island trailing their branches in the lake. Above them, the sky was a pale, silky blue.

"I don't want to die," said Hortensia, after they had

sat in silence for some minutes. "I want to live forever. This is a world I can never ever tire of."

Vinetta did not know what to say, did not know how to respond to such intensity.

"We speak only of what we know," she said at last. "There are myriads of things we can't know."

She looked at Hortensia before adding, "The unknown might be wonderful too."

Hortensia, already uncomfortable at having said so much, said briskly, "I think we should be going home now. Baby needs her tea."

Vinetta pushed the pram out of the park and up the hill, but when they came to the main road again, Hortensia took over.

They walked on for some minutes in silence. Then Hortensia said, "I think I may have to spend a little time in my cupboard, Vinetta. Just a day or two. I need to think."

Vinetta looked embarrassed.

"You mean you would like to have a short holiday?" she said with a struggle. To remember that Hortensia had once lived in the hall cupboard was surely taboo.

Hortensia gave her a bitter smile.

"No, Vinetta," she said, "I do mean my cupboard. The pretends are all over, haven't you realized that?"

They turned the corner into Brocklehurst Grove.

"I think it might be better if you walked on ahead now," she said. "It's nearly time for the children to come out of school. The street may be a little too busy for two of us together."

* * *

The weather grew warmer and the days grew longer, but the two friends never ventured out together again. For some reason that neither could quite pinpoint, the outing ultimately felt like a failure.

❧ 14 ❧

Preparations

The pages turned on the calendar . . . April . . .
May . . . June . . . July . . . Some preparations were
made, but mostly life went on as if there were no deadline. On the first of September, Magnus called a meeting
in his room for all but the youngest members of the
family. Joshua was at work, but Magnus had come
round to Soobie's point of view. There was no point in
troubling Joshua before it became necessary for him to
leave his job at Sydenham's. He would not argue, but
he would not cooperate, and sometimes a sullen silence
is harder to cope with than rage.

Magnus was sitting up in bed, at least five pillows
supporting him. In his left hand he held a notebook
open at a page on which he had written a long and
detailed list. In his right, a pen was held poised ready
to tick off each item.

"Now," he said when everyone was seated, "we
have just one month to go. It must be a time of earnest
effort. Let us consider everything that needs to be
done."

He turned to Tulip.

"Finances first. What have you done about them?"

Tulip told him of her strategy. She was pleased to

tell him that she had realized all of their investments, and the large sums produced had been invested in various Building Societies. Everything done by post and telephone of course, everything checked and double-checked. She had not missed a single thing. All Magnus had to do was to tick down the page.

When Tulip explained about her fail-safe procedure, he looked scornful.

"A year and a day! Hmph! I don't see any point in that," he said, holding the pen poised high in the air, since these were items not included on *his* list of necessities. "You might as well have left straightforward letters. Whatever we may need in the hereafter, supposing there is one, money will not be part of it. And if you think there could be a last minute reprieve, think again. This premonition is too strong for anything so trivial."

Tulip refused to be drawn into an argument. She went on to tell of the arrangements with the solicitors—their own and those who still administered the Loftus estate.

"I have done exactly as you told me," she said. "Should the situation arise, it will be made quite clear to the firm of Cromarty, Varley and Thynne that this house and everything in it is to be handed over to the Gladstones. Our own solicitors will know exactly what to do after reading my instructions, such instructions to be read on and not before the first of December, unless I write and ask to have them returned unopened. That will give me plenty of time to get the letter back. This is all a game, of course. But I have played it straight. I just hope you appreciate my efforts."

She looked disdainful. Work done, to be undone. She had made profits along the way, but that was incidental.

Still, it was an achievement and not one of the others could have done so much.

Magnus shrugged. If his wife still believed in life after the first of October, nothing else he could say was going to change her views. The main thing was to get the preparations made. "And I have arranged for the household bills to be paid by direct debit from the bank for up to six months after our departure," Tulip continued. "That will give the Gladstones all the time they need to take over. We would not want to leave debts. Our solicitor will continue to be paid in the same way till the accounts are closed."

This was better, thought Magnus. No matter what she might say to the contrary, she was sounding less of a disbeliever.

"Will there be enough money in the current account?" asked Magnus.

"More than enough. That account will remain open for a year. Interest from the Building Societies will be paid directly into it. When it is closed any sum remaining will be paid over to charity. That too is in a sealed letter to be held unopened by the bank manager. I have also asked him to send out no bank statements until requested. You have put me to a lot of trouble, Magnus."

She looked at him critically, but she did want him to be pleased. On a purely intellectual level, she had enjoyed solving the puzzles Magnus had set. To go the extra step and fully believe in his nonsense was something she could not manage.

Next Sir Magnus turned to Vinetta. He found her

place on his list. Her outside business had included making children's clothes for a boutique in Castledean.

"You've stopped supplying clothes to that shop in town, I hope?" he said.

"Long since," said Vinetta. "I was not happy with the prices she was prepared to pay. Finishing with her had nothing to do with our present problem."

Then it was Miss Quigley's turn.

"I think you should stack your canvases in the garden shed," said Sir Magnus. That may have sounded heartless, but he went on to redeem himself with his next words. "You are as good a painter as many a professional. If the canvases are hidden away they will be found some time later. They will be a mystery. Their intrinsic worth might be recognized by someone of artistic discernment. Cover them well so that the damp does not harm them. The remainder of your paints and paraphernalia can go in the bin. And do make sure that you return your library books."

Hortensia was astounded that he knew about the visits she paid to the public library. She should not have been. Not much escaped Sir Magnus. He might spend all of his days in bed, but he had his informers.

Magnus turned to Soobie.

"I have no outside interests, Granpa," said Soobie before his grandfather could speak. "I jog in the evening. Weather permitting, I shall most probably go jogging on the thirtieth of September. But I shall stay at home on the first of October. That should satisfy you."

Granpa nodded. He looked down at the notebook.

"That seems to cover everything, except that my son must hand in his notice at that confounded warehouse.

You must see to that, Vinetta. He takes more notice of you than of anybody else.''

The meeting was about to adjourn when Pilbeam asked a final question.

''If we are really going to cease to live when October comes, it will be important for us to come to some decision as to where we should be when it happens.''

They all looked at her. Possibilities flitted through their minds. The attic was the obvious place. It was there that Appleby had ceased to live. It was there in fact that they had all first come to life, though of the precise moment they had no recollection. All birth is ''but a sleep and a forgetting,'' even for rag dolls. The attic had been their store cupboard, with dolls lying neatly in rows in the half that had long been empty. And though not one of them really remembered that, they were in silent agreement that the attic was the one place they would not consider. Fate might be about to claim them, but they had no intention of meeting her halfway. And, besides, if this were just an old man's folly, a gathering up there under the rafters on a dark autumn evening would be uncomfortable and ridiculous.

Miss Quigley had been very subdued for the whole of this meeting. Ceasing to live meant dying, and dying was morbidly horrible. She would rather not talk about it. But one thing she felt sure of, if she were going to die, she would not want to die in Sir Magnus's room.

''I shall spend that evening in the hall cupboard,'' she said. ''Then if it really does happen, I shall feel safe.''

''Safe, but alone, Hortensia,'' said Vinetta. ''That is not how it should be. We must all be together.''

''You shall come to my room on the stroke of seven.

Nothing will happen before then," said Granpa, hardly conscious of what he was saying until he had said it. He did not bother to explain it away. "Don't ask me how I know," he said. "I just do."

"We can't be found here," said Miss Quigley, ingenuity coming to her rescue. "It is not fitting that the master bedroom should be found full of dolls. If we are going to be just dolls with no life in us, we must be found in a cupboard."

"We couldn't all fit in *your* cupboard," Vinetta protested. "There's barely room for one."

"No," said Hortensia. "We are very big dolls. We would need a doll room rather than a doll cupboard, but it would not need to be as large a room as this."

"So what do you suggest?" asked Magnus.

"Either of the rooms that used to be guest rooms long ago—Pilbeam's room or Soobie's."

It was Vinetta who had the last word.

"No," she said, "neither of those. There is one room in this house sacred to a dead daughter. We shall join her there. That will be the doll room."

❧ 15 ❧

Problems

*H*ortensia was noticeably quiet. It was rare for her to be so silent. She and Vinetta were sitting in the day nursery next afternoon. Googles was asleep. Vinetta looked anxiously at her friend and ally.

"There's something wrong," she said. "What is it? Why aren't you talking to me?"

Hortensia shrugged. "There's nothing to say," she said. "There are no plans left to make. There is no future."

But Vinetta sensed that there was more to it than that. Something was niggling Miss Quigley, something other than their general situation. Vinetta was sewing a tape back onto one of Googles's bibs. She put her work aside and brought all her concentration to bear on whatever problem Hortensia was nursing.

"Come on, Hortensia," she said. "I know there's more to it than that. You have hardly spoken to me since yesterday, and you look so worried anyone would know there's something wrong. You are not much good at hiding your feelings."

Hortensia looked embarrassed.

"You'll think me foolish," she said, "but I really can't help it. I would if I could, but I honestly can't."

"Can't help what?" said Vinetta.

"On the day, on the first of October," Hortensia began awkwardly, "I don't want to go into Appleby's room. I just don't want to."

"Why ever not? We'll all be together, all of us. That must be right."

"I don't want to see Appleby," said Hortensia. "I want to remember her as she was. I don't want to see her lying dead."

Vinetta understood. It was the old phobia, the reason why her friend had refused to paint a picture of her dead daughter. It had not mattered much then. Now it did.

"I think," said Vinetta, "that we should go and see her now, this minute. She is lying peaceful and there is nothing about her to fear. The only way you are going to know that is by coming with me to see her."

"No!" said Hortensia sharply. "Please don't ask."

"Yes," said Vinetta. "I wouldn't ask it at all, but it is for your own good. Come now."

She took Hortensia by the arm and pulled her firmly to her feet. Hortensia was propelled out of the door and to the bottom of the staircase. She did not resist but her whole stance bespoke an unwillingness to go.

"This is unkind of you, Vinetta," she said. "You know how I feel. I'm not just afraid. I am terrified."

It was a pathetic admission but Vinetta's resolve did not weaken. They walked slowly up the two flights of stairs. Hortensia leaned heavily on the banister. Vinetta held one hand under her other elbow.

"You'll be surprised at how unfrightened you'll be when you see her," she said.

Vinetta opened Appleby's door. The room was sweet and clean and pretty. Hortensia tried not to look across at the bed. Vinetta, unwavering, led her toward it. Then they both stood and looked down at the lifeless figure of Appleby. Slowly, the expression on Hortensia's face changed. She reached out one hand and touched a lock of red hair.

"She is lovely and so peaceful," said Hortensia. "She could just be sleeping."

It was some minutes before she added, "I'm glad you made me come."

"And if Magnus is right," said Vinetta in a quiet, gentle voice, "that is how we will all be after the first of next month. It is not so very bad a fate."

Hortensia stroked Appleby's hair back from her brow.

"But who knows what comes after?" she said.

"That surely is the mystery," said Vinetta, "and the wonder."

Tulip had an entirely different problem. She did not believe that the first of October would be any other than the day before the second of October. She agreed to all the palaver of preparing and assembling in Appleby's room, but she felt sure that it would be nothing but a damp squib. Life would go on, and all the preparations would have to be unraveled. Then, just as she had satisfied herself that everything that had been done could be undone, another thought occurred to her. What if, improbable though it was, life really did leave them? It might not leave forever. There was a time before they had lived, a time long, long ago. Then they must have been inanimate rag dolls. What happened to bring them to life? Tulip did not know. No one could know. But if it happened before, it could happen again.

The thought sent her into a fever of activity that ended with her hurrying to her husband's bedside. She was even slightly breathless when she sat down in her usual chair. A flustered Tulip was a rarity.

"Magnus," she said, "you must know that, in spite of all my doubts, I have done absolutely everything you have asked."

"Yes," said Magnus. "I have no complaints."

"Then I would like you to do something very special for me."

"Yes?" said Magnus, giving her a cautious look.

From her knitting bag she produced a small package, well wrapped in brown paper.

"You remember, all those years ago, when we first came to life?"

"Yes," said Magnus.

"Well, we were very glad of the cache of money we found in Aunt Kate's workbox. It tided us over very well till we got into the way of creating our own wealth."

"True," said Magnus, "and you made a brilliant job of it. Credit where credit's due."

"All my fail-safes are to do with my firm belief that we shall never die. I want one more. Just in case we do die, and months from now or even years from now we come to life again, I want us to have another cache of money."

Magnus considered well what she was saying before he replied.

"It won't be as simple as that," he said. "I don't

believe that we ever will be restored to life. When it is over, it is over. But, suppose something of the sort does happen, how do you know that the hidden money would be where you could find it? The Gladstones will take over. They would probably find any money left in the house. We did! And they may not leave us undisturbed in the doll room. After the first of October, everything is beyond our control.''

"They won't destroy us," said Tulip shrewdly. "We are much too well made. So what I propose to do is to give you charge of this bundle of notes, and one or two other things, which will be hidden on your person.''

"Without wishing to be indelicate," said Magnus, "I feel sure that whoever looks after us will want to change our clothing from time to time. There will be nothing hidden.''

"That," said Tulip, "is why the money must be hidden on you. Well, not on you, but in you.''

Magnus, as well he might, looked horrified. The look Tulip gave him in return was kind, but firm.

"Your feet are neatly sewn," she said, "but I could undo the stitching, remove some of the stuffing and wedge the bundle in place.''

"What about your own feet?" said Magnus, outraged. "What about Joshua's feet? Or Vinetta's?''

"They are not bulky enough. And I also think that it is a decided advantage that your feet are purple. It gives them an air of inviolable eccentricity.''

"Thank you," said Magnus drily. "It makes a change for my feet to be inoffensive.'' He still remembered how squeamish Albert Pond had been about the foot that hung over the side of the bed. He still remembered how Tulip had insisted upon covering it with the quilt.

"Besides," said Tulip, "you are the head of the household. It is fitting that you should take charge of our hidden treasure."

After a few blank refusals, backed up with various expletives, Magnus finally gave way. Tulip played her trump card. She threatened to leave home on the day of days if he would not agree to her terms.

"After all I have done for you," she said, "it is a very small thing to ask you to do for me—for us. If you won't do it, I shall walk out of the front door on the first of October and stay away till your charade is over."

Magnus knew her well enough to suspect that she meant every word. And he could not rely upon the rest of the household to bundle her into the doll room when the final hour drew nigh!

"Very well. Have your way. Get on with it then," he said, raising his foot and placing it on the arm of the chair as on an operating table.

Tulip brought her workbox and deftly unpicked about six inches of stitching. She removed a wad of padding, shoved the bundle of money into the hole, and stitched the gap so perfectly that no one would have known it had been there.

"Satisfied?" said Magnus, letting his foot hang limp again.

"Of course," said Tulip. "I don't know what all the fuss was about. It was simplicity itself."

"Grave goods," Magnus muttered. "Idiotic grave goods."

❦ 16 ❧

The Thirtieth of September

As the month grew older the doomed dolls became more and more conscious of how slowly time could move. Minutes seemed to last for hours. The women, wondering whether their actions had any point at all, cleaned the house from top to bottom, laying fresh paper on shelves, sweeping into every neglected corner. Pilbeam, a secret writer, destroyed everything she had ever written. Soobie put all of his books in order. Miss Quigley folded dozens of baby clothes and packed them into boxes. Tulip filled black bags with things that needed to be thrown away before the strangers should come in and take over. She still did not believe the worst would happen but she was not averse to a good spring-clean: when it was all over the house would be more orderly than it had been for years!

On Monday, the thirtieth of September, Sir Magnus called his last conference. Poopie and Wimpey were not invited. They had been told nothing of the coming crisis. That was Vinetta's firm decision. Joshua was not present either. He was at work.

"Magnus wants us all to be there," Vinetta said. "He'll be annoyed."

But Joshua already had on his outdoor clothes. He

gave his wife a look of inexorable stubbornness. What he really thought about it all, he never said. He would not argue, or interfere with whatever any of the others wanted to do. But, but, but, *but* he was not prepared to let it make one whit of difference to his own life.

"It's Tuesday tomorrow. I'll be home all day and all night," he said. "If Father wants me to come to Appleby's room, I'll come. But tonight I go to work."

The first thing Magnus said when they were ready to begin the conference was, "Where's Joshua? He's not still going to that warehouse, is he?"

"Yes," said Vinetta. "I have tried all ways to persuade him to hand in his notice, but he wouldn't. I even tried to talk him into staying at home tonight, but to no avail. You know what he's like, Magnus. He never argues. He just won't listen."

Magnus gave Tulip a sour look. She was the sower of doubt. It was all her fault.

"So," he said, "he doesn't believe it's going to happen?"

"Deep down," said Vinetta, "I think he might. He has agreed to come to Appleby's room tomorrow. He never says what he believes. He never has. You should know that."

"Have you not explained . . ." began Magnus, but then he changed his mind and did not bother to finish the sentence.

"It won't matter anyway," said Vinetta. "He'll be here tomorrow. That's the main thing."

They went over again all the preparations they had made, all the eventualities they had covered.

"What about the young ones?" said Magnus.

"I'll see to them tomorrow morning," said Vinetta. "That will be soon enough. I am hoping they will remember nothing of your Christmas outburst. The less time they have to think about tomorrow, the better."

Miss Quigley, a little shyly, produced a square board for them to inspect. It was polished wood, walnut veneer, with a black scrolled border. In bold letters in the center it had the words:

DOLL ROOM

"I made this for the door," she said. "It will make it clearer that the room is special, even before anyone enters."

Sir Magnus, who could be gracious on occasion, took the board in both hands and lay back to admire it.

"A fine piece of work, Miss Quigley. Very fine. Joshua must fix it in place when he comes home tomorrow morning."

"I have been thinking too," said Vinetta. "It might be a good idea to leave a note for the incoming people, explaining who we are. They are bound to be puzzled."

"Who are we?" said Magnus. "What are we?"

Tulip recognized his words as an echo of something he had said long ago.

"At best we are ourselves," she said, "living and breathing and very special. At worst we are the finest rag dolls ever made."

"That is why we must leave a note, a sort of explanation. It need not be long," said Vinetta. "We can leave it on Appleby's dressing table, propped up so that it will be found straightaway."

"And who would be the supposed writer of this note?" said Magnus.

"Aunt Kate. Who else? It will have been left there by the mysterious Mennym family—a note found by them nearly half a century ago, a note kept and treasured as they have kept and treasured the dolls."

"So," said Magnus, warming to the idea, "these Gladstones will never know that we *are* the Mennyms. They will think . . ."

"They can think what they like," said Vinetta. "They will never suspect the truth."

Pilbeam's writing was thought most nearly to resemble Kate's own hand. Notepaper was brought from the old desk in the breakfast room, and a real fountain pen. Pilbeam sat ready to take down the words. She looked at her mother expectantly.

"Write this," said Vinetta. " 'The dolls in this room are my people . . .' " She spoke slowly, pausing to allow her daughter to write clearly. " 'Work of my hands and of my heart . . .' "

Pilbeam wrote and waited for what would come next. Vinetta looked round at every face in the room, each one so dear to her.

"Yes, Mum?" said Pilbeam, waiting for whatever instruction Vinetta meant to pass on to the newcomers. It was surprisingly short.

In a lower voice, she said, "Next put—'Please, love them.' And sign it 'Kate Penshaw.' "

There was a silence. Then Magnus said gruffly, "It doesn't say much."

"It says all it needs to say," said Vinetta.

The page was put into a large envelope. On the outside, Soobie wrote the words:

FOR THE NEXT OWNERS OF THIS HOUSE:
A LETTER PRESERVED FOR FORTY-SEVEN YEARS.
KATE PENSHAW'S DYING WISH
WHICH WE HAVE FAITHFULLY OBSERVED.

The meeting ended and Soobie went out into the night. For hours he jogged around all the familiar places, the road that passed three churches, the park, and the moor where they had sledged in winter. He turned and came into town again, made his way along the streets where he had once sought for Appleby in the rain, went as far as the Theatre Royal, then turned down toward the river, crossed over the Dean Bridge and back over the Low Bridge, up Sandy Bank and across the marketplace. In the dead of night, the streets were almost empty. Soobie had the freedom of the city. He was filled with love for Castledean.

I can't imagine dying, he thought. I don't think I would know *how* to die.

❖ 17 ❖

Tuesday Morning

The post brought the customary first-of-October letter from Cromarty, Varley and Thynne. Tulip took it straight to Magnus's room, waking her husband at an unusually early hour.

"Well?" he said sharply. "What do you want?"

Then he remembered what day it was. There was no point in being cross. Hours spent sleeping were not so precious if all the hours of the hereafter were to pass in slumber. He saw the letter in Tulip's hand and knew at once what it was.

"Throw it away," he said. "Put it in with the rest of the rubbish."

"Nonsense," said Tulip. "It is the declaration. You will have to sign it."

"Do you understand nothing? Signing it would be pointless. It would be worse than pointless. If we rushed it out to the solicitor today, what do you think would happen?"

"We would be left untroubled for another year perhaps," said Tulip.

"We would be left neglected in an empty house. Dust would cover us and heaven knows what harm the place might come to. I love this house, Tulip. After my departure from this life, I want people to come in and care for it. I want them to love it too. And they will. They couldn't help loving it.''

''The Gladstones? After all you've said about them!'' said Tulip bluntly.

''Hobson's choice,'' said Magnus. ''They're better than nobody.''

''You could be wrong about us dying,'' said Tulip. ''What if we are still alive tomorrow?''

''I won't be wrong,'' said Magnus, ''but if it will make you any happier, let me say this—tomorrow will be just one day later than usual. Hold on to the declaration if you must. Tomorrow, if I am alive, I shall be delighted to sign it, seal it and have it delivered.''

The letter that accompanied the official form made no reference at all to birth certificates. Tulip noted that and was glad. Tomorrow it would be all over. One way . . . or another.

When Joshua returned from work, he had his usual breakfast with Vinetta. She made him an omelette with make-believe eggs and served him toast and marmalade. He ate the phantom meal with relish and thanked Vinetta for it. She told him about the notice Hortensia had made and he agreed to fix it in place.

''Now I am going to bed,'' he said, after he had done the job and put his tools away. ''That walk home wasn't pleasant today. It's very windy outside.''

''You will remember about this evening,'' said Vinetta anxiously.

''I'll be there,'' said Joshua. ''I have said I would. Don't worry.''

*   *   *

When Vinetta went to waken Poopie and Wimpey, she had her plans already laid. Poopie first. She went to his room where he was lying still asleep with one arm around the toy rabbit he called Paddy Black. Vinetta went to his wardrobe and from the very back she took out a pair of short gray trousers, a maroon school blazer and a little peaked cap. From a drawer she took a gray shirt and a maroon and gray striped tie.

"Poopie," she said. "Poopie. Wake up, dear. I want to talk to you."

Poopie sat up in bed, looking bewildered. He shook his head and then ran his fingers through his hair.

"What d'you want?" he said crossly. "It's too soon to get up."

"I want to explain to you about today," said his mother. "It is a very special day."

"Is it?" said Poopie, trying to come fully awake.

"Yes," said Vinetta. "It is special because this evening we are all to go to Appleby's room. Granpa has said we must. He believes that Aunt Kate is coming to pay us a visit. She will want to see us dressed just as we were when she left. So today I would like you to wear your school uniform and pretend that you are a real schoolboy. That should be a nice pretend. You won't need to do any lessons, of course. We can pretend that it is a half-holiday. But those are the clothes you must wear."

"Yuk!" said Poopie. "I hate them. You know I do! I thought I'd finished with them years ago."

"Your grandfather particularly wants you to wear

them," said Vinetta firmly. "It is a dressing-up game. And it is just for one day. Just to please Granpa."

She did not explain that the clothes had to be worn not for Kate but for the incoming Gladstones. All of them would have to wear old-fashioned clothes to fit the period when their life first began. It would not have to be a rigid rule. The dolls, being cared for, would have had new clothing over the years. But to keep to an older style would seem more authentic. Pilbeam would be wearing her Fair Isle jumper, gray pleated skirt and white bobby socks. Soobie had rebelled against being forced to wear anything other than his tracksuit. The ladies, it must be said, found no problem. Their style of dress had hardly changed in all their years.

Wimpey was very easy. She looked old-fashioned anyway with her hair in bunches and her big bows of ribbon. Vinetta got out an old, blue-checked gingham dress with a big sash that tied at the back.

"Oh, Mum!" said Wimpey. "It's ages since I wore that dress!"

"It's just for today," said Vinetta and was about to explain Granpa's wishes when Wimpey interrupted to say, "I love it. I always loved it. Why can't I wear it every day?"

Vinetta hugged her and said no more.

Miss Quigley had work to do, her own special work.

First of all she tipped all of her spare paints into a rubbish bag. Soobie saw her taking it onto the landing and said, "Can I help?"

Miss Quigley smiled weakly and said, "These have to go out for the binmen. They'll be coming tomorrow, so everything will be well out of the way before, well, before you know what."

"I'll take the bag for you," said Soobie. "Is there anything else I can help with?"

Miss Quigley looked doubtful.

"I don't want to impose," she said. "It isn't fair. . . ."

"But?" said Soobie with a smile.

"No, I must do it myself," said Miss Quigley firmly. "You must have many other things to do."

"I have nothing to do," said Soobie, "and if this is really to be our last day, I would like to spend it being of some use to somebody. I'll put this bag outside and then return for orders."

In less than a minute he was back at Miss Quigley's room, helping her to pack her canvases in protective paper and plastic bags.

"Now what?" he said when they were all stacked up in the hall.

"They are to be hidden in the back of the garden shed," said Miss Quigley. "But please don't trouble. I can do it myself."

The canvases were bulky and numerous; the corridor was two floors up. Soobie knew that Miss Quigley had the determination to carry out the task, even if it took her all day; but he could see further. He could see past her determination into her weariness, her soul quailing at the thought of all those trips up and down two flights of stairs, out through the back door and across the garden to the shed.

"Go to Googles," he said gently. "Spend time with her."

"But . . ." protested Miss Quigley.

"No buts," said Soobie, taking one parcel under each arm. "Go downstairs to Googles. I will look after these."

As the day went on, the wind dropped, the sun shone and it became almost warm. Poopie, uncomfortable in his uniform, sat on the back step with his toy rabbit, Paddy Black, by his side. Wimpey sat on the swing, nursing Polly, her American doll, still her favorite no matter what other dolls might be added to her collection. Soobie finished his task and returned to his seat by the window. In her bedroom Pilbeam made sure that everything was neat and tidy.

Vinetta and Hortensia sat together in the nursery where Googles was playing a particularly lively game in her playpen. And Tulip? Tulip spent the day in Appleby's room, bringing in and arranging stools and chairs. Before the light faded, she went to Magnus, helped him into his dressing gown and slippers and took him to the armchair she had placed by Appleby's bed. Seeing him sitting there she could almost believe that his predictions might come true. Almost, but not quite.

"It has been a very long day," said Vinetta as she switched on the light and drew the nursery curtains.

"A long day," said Hortensia, "but a short life."

At six-thirty, the whole family began to prepare for the seven o'clock deadline. In one way, it had hung over the day so much that they were glad to do so. But in addition, it must be said, not one of them would have had the temerity to disobey Sir Magnus's strict instructions.

The television in the lounge was switched off and unplugged. Miss Quigley, hearing the others moving about, came into the hall with Googles in her arms. Soobie and Pilbeam joined them.

"Anyone else down here?" said Vinetta.

"No," said Soobie. "Poopie and Wimpey are in their own rooms. I think Granny must be with Granpa. Dad went upstairs about ten minutes ago."

"Good," said Vinetta. "The next thing is to lock up and see that everything is right on this floor."

They locked and bolted the back door. The front door was locked, but left unbolted. Pilbeam had been about to draw the bolt when her mother stopped her.

"If things come to pass as Granpa has foretold," said Vinetta, "someone is going to have to come in from the outside with a key. We wouldn't want them to have to break the door down."

All of the ground floor lights were extinguished. The front curtains were opened, but not too wide. When day came again, a house with all of the curtains closed might look odd to outsiders.

They all proceeded to the floor above.

"It's time to go," said Vinetta, looking in at the big front bedroom where Joshua lay half-asleep. "Straighten the bed cover. Put out the table lamp and open the curtains."

Joshua got up and did exactly as he was told.

Poopie was called out from his room. His toys had all been put away in their cupboards. Everything was in a tidier state than it had been for many a long year.

Vinetta, looking in earlier in the day, had been appalled at the mess. So Poopie was told that his room might be inspected by Aunt Kate when she came to visit. The idea of a kit inspection had led him to spend the past two hours tidying his room till everything was all ship-shape and Bristol fashion. It was like a game of soldiers—or sailors!

When Wimpey came out of her room carrying Polly, the American doll, Poopie took one look at her and dived back into this own room. A rummage in the cupboard and he emerged again with Paddy Black under his arm.

Eight living rag dolls formed a puzzled group on the landing. Even Googles, wriggling in Hortensia's arms, looked bewildered. Vinetta ushered them up ahead of her, but Joshua insisted upon going last.

The lights were extinguished on this floor too. By Joshua.

Next, each room on the top landing was checked and left in darkness. They came at last to Appleby's door. The plaque Miss Quigley had made was fixed neatly to the center panel. Poopie and Wimpey read it and were puzzled.

"It is part of the game," said Vinetta and felt guilty, guilty, guilty. But what else could she say? What else could she do? There was still the faint hope that it might be no more than a foolish pretend. They would sit and wait and nothing would happen. Poopie would end up in a tired tantrum, calling it a *daft* game, a *right* load of rubbish. But if they all lived through this night, thought Vinetta, oh he could call it anything he liked!

They went into the room and Tulip told them where to sit.

"Now," said Magnus, "you must switch off this light and open the curtains. The moon will give us all the illumination we will need in the short time before—"

Vinetta, seated on the settle (brought from Pilbeam's room), Poopie one side of her, Wimpey the other, interrupted him.

"—in the time before Kate comes to see us," she said, hugging both children. "This is like magic. Who knows what might happen?"

❧ 18 ❧

Waiting

The window of Appleby's room overlooked the back garden, no street lamps there, no lights from other houses. Far away across the hedge and beyond unkempt gardens, the Georgian houses in the old terrace, ghostly neighbors, were deserted and derelict. Only the pale moonlight saved the "doll room" from total darkness.

The seating arrangements were very precise, giving each one all the support he or she would need if death should really come. Joshua had been directed by Tulip to a carver chair brought up from the dining room. It was wedged between the wardrobe and the settle where Vinetta sat with the younger twins. To the other side of the settle, on a velvet pouffe jammed up against the armrest, sat Pilbeam. Miss Quigley nursed Googles in a chair placed in the corner furthest away from Appleby's bed. Closest to the bed were Sir Magnus in the big armchair and Granny Tulip on a basket bedroom chair supported by three large cushions. Soobie had another carver chair just by the door.

The luminous points of the clock on the wall showed how the minutes ticked by. Seven o'clock became seven-thirty and nothing happened. The family waited in silence.

It became too much for Poopie. He held onto Paddy Black and gave a quiet giggle into his velvet fur. It was like playing hide-and-seek, the whole family sitting there crammed into one little room in the darkness. Vinetta shushed him but sympathized. What were they all doing here? It said much for Sir Magnus's authority that he had got them this far. If any of them had ever believed in the coming of the end, and to be honest some of them had, their belief dwindled as they sat there feeling more and more silly.

"Will Aunt Kate be coming soon?" whispered Wimpey.

Joshua heard her and grunted.

"Just wait," Vinetta whispered in reply. "She might not come after all. We can't be sure."

The waiting went on for another hour. The odd word was passed in a whisper and each whisper elicited a frown from Magnus.

We are pretending to be dolls, thought Vinetta, and the thought made *her* feel giggly in a nervous way. Only the smallest of sounds escaped her lips and only Joshua noticed. He looked round the room. Stuffed dummies, he thought, but felt no inclination to laugh. What will happen will happen. Waiting here is stupid.

"I've had enough of this," he said loudly. "At least, let's have the light on."

He sprang up from his chair, but before he could do anything his father yelled at him, "Don't move another step, Joshua. Sit down and wait. Don't you dare do anything. Am I the head of this household, or am I not?"

Joshua was about to argue, but Vinetta pulled him by the sleeve, and made him sit down.

"There's no point in arguing," she said. "If he is wrong, time will prove it. Even if it takes a few hours, we must give him that time. If he is right, then we are where we should be."

It was Poopie's turn to protest. He stood up, still clutching Paddy Black.

"A few *hours*. You must be mad. You must all be mad. We've been here for ages and ages already. We can't wait forever. She might never come. It's just a game."

"We can wait," said his grandfather in slow tones like a preacher speaking from the pulpit, "and we will. And it is not Kate we are waiting for, young man. It is Destiny."

Poopie sat back baffled. Wimpey trembled and hugged her doll tightly. She did not know what the word *destiny* meant, but she felt instinctively that it was something to fear.

Magnus's dramatic insistence on declaring what he believed to be the truth had the effect of quashing any thoughts of rebellion. Even Tulip, sitting close to him, stifled an inclination to protest. Vinetta was angry, but this time it was Joshua's turn to restrain *her,* to reach over and grip her shoulder.

"Steady," he said quietly, "steady. Let him have the time he needs. You can chide him later."

So they all sat there, waiting, like passengers in a railway carriage wondering when the train will leave the station. There should be something like the shunting of an engine, the slow turning of wheels, some indication that the journey is about to begin . . .

Joshua sat back in his chair, folded his arms and attempted to sleep. His chin sank to his chest but sleep would not come. In a little while, Poopie and Wimpey both cuddled into Vinetta and really did sleep. Miss Quigley dozed, holding Googles firmly in her arms. Tulip lay back on her cushions and went off into a reverie, making plans for all she would have to do in the next few days to put everything right again—and this included looking after Magnus, who might be expected to suffer acute embarrassment when dawn came and found them no different from the day before.

Two people in that room were fully alert. Magnus was looking over Appleby's bed toward the window where the moon was dipping in the sky and would soon shine directly in. What did he expect? Kate to come and summon their wraiths to join her? To see the ghost in whom he had once expressed scornful disbelief? How *does* a rag doll die?

Soobie, well shadowed in his seat by the door, thought of his dead sister and wondered—*How* does a rag doll die? He remembered the door in the attic. As the minutes turned to hours, he noticed how still and silent the others all were. Even the whispers had stopped entirely. He thought again of the door in the attic and he made up his mind to go and see. Moving silently, warily watching the back of Granpa's chair, he turned the door handle and cautiously opened the room door. Edging it just far enough open, he slipped out into the hall and closed it behind him.

He walked carefully along the dark landing toward

the attic stairs. The staircase was lighter because it had a small uncurtained window that faced toward the front of the house where there were street lamps, and the glow of the town hung in the sky. Soobie climbed the staircase, wincing at every creak he made on the bare boards and hoping that the sound would not carry. He was as cautious going into the attic as he had been in leaving the bedroom below. No lights. It was possible that Granpa could be right, and if they really were all going to die, the house must be left unlit as it would be if a real family had quit the premises.

The attic was darker than the stairs, but there was enough illumination from the skylights for Soobie to make his way to the rocking chair without falling over. He sat down and looked toward the mysterious door. If death comes now, he thought, then I shall die alone. Apt fate for a blue Mennym, a misfit even in his own odd family. He did not want to be found with the rest of them. He would much prefer never to be found at all. But would it happen? Would they really cease to live?

He lay stretched out in the rocking chair and rocked slowly back and forward. It will happen, he thought. And rocked. It won't happen, he thought. And rocked again. It can't happen, he thought, and thrust his feet onto the footstool, bringing the chair to a halt. Across the attic, the length of the house away, the mystic door was so deep in shadow it was practically invisible.

In the room below, the moonlight crept in over the bed and shone on Appleby's face. Her grandfather, just beginning to nod, looked up with a jerk.

What he saw brought a strangled squeak to the little voice box in his throat. Appleby's head was moving!

Her face was turning slowly toward him. He found himself gazing into unseeing green glass eyes. The doll in the bed groaned softly. Quiet, so quiet it was, but in that silent room loud enough to arouse everyone. They all sat up straight and looked toward Appleby with a feeling that can only be described as terror. Even Vinetta was terrified. The twins let go of their toys and dug their fingers into their mother's arms. Paddy Black and Polly clattered to the floor. No one gave them a thought. All eyes were fixed on the bed bathed in moonlight.

Then the figure of Appleby sat bolt upright. She did not look at any of them. She seemed not to know that they were there. Her arms rose up and stretched toward the ceiling. In a clear voice, she called out, "Kate!" The single word came out in a slow and piercing wail.

In the attic, at that moment, Soobie saw the far door swing slowly open and a milky white light begin to spill across the wood floor. Then, then . . . stillness.

Appleby fell back onto her pillows, as dead as she had ever been. The others in the room gave one last gasp, and ceased to live. Their bodies swayed to left and right, settling in helpless poses. Bereft of their spirit, they were just an odd assortment of rag dolls, indistinguishable in kind from the stuffed toy rabbit that lay on the floor.

Kate Penshaw was gone.

The Mennyms were all alone.

Part Two

Please, love them . . .

❧ 19 ❧

News for Jennifer

News of the departure of the Mennym family reached the Gladstones by letter on Friday the thirteenth of December. It was a very short, formal invitation to call at the office of Cromarty, Varley and Thynne to sign some papers and to accept the keys to Number 5 Brocklehurst Grove, "which premises have, on the instructions of the previous owner, been inspected by an independent surveyor and found to be in good order."

Jennifer was alone in the house when she read the letter. Her first reaction was one of apprehension and dismay. It was over a year since the letter requesting birth certificates had been sent and received its coldly civil reply. Jennifer had been more than content to forget about the whole business. But the memory of it was there at the back of her mind, waiting to pounce. It made her look carefully for hidden meanings.

Why had the Mennyms insisted upon a survey? To Jennifer that suggested hostility. They obviously wanted to show her how well they had cared for the house during their years of stewardship. You have driven us out, it said, but we have left with dignity.

"We'll have to go and see it," said Tom when he read the letter. "When shall we pick up the keys?"

Jennifer pushed a stray wisp of hair back from her brow and answered him tersely.

"After New Year," she said. "I'll ring up and make an appointment. No one wants to see people just before the holidays."

Tom looked at her and he knew what she was thinking. Years of practice had made him an expert. He smiled.

"You're probably right," he said, "and another week or two will give you time to get used to the idea. But try not to wonder about the Mennyms. Where they have gone and why they have gone is none of our business."

Jennifer bit her lip. She hesitated before saying, "You don't think it could because we asked for the birth certificates?" She stared at the letter as if it could give her some sort of clue. "I'd hate to think we'd driven them away. Brocklehurst Grove was their home. It has been their home for goodness knows how many years. I probably wasn't even born when they first went to live with Aunt Kate."

Tom grasped Jennifer firmly by both shoulders.

"Listen," he said, "don't let your imagination run away with you. People are not so easily driven away. The Mennyms have gone and, I do assure you, their going had nothing whatsoever to do with your letter. Don't look for what's not there."

"I am pleased, you know," said Jennifer, looking down at the letter. "We do need more space. And by the time we sell *this* house, we'll be better off than we've ever been. But, you're right—it does take getting used to."

"Why don't you ring your mother?" said Tom.

"She'll be delighted. Family property returning to the family . . ."

"Not yet," said Jennifer. "I don't want to tell any of them yet. Let's just wait till after Christmas."

"If you say so," said Tom, "but it seems mean. This is good news. I would have thought you'd want to share it. Leave the keys till after Christmas if that's what you want to do, but I think you should tell the family about the letter. There is no point in keeping it a secret. I doubt if you could manage it anyway."

Jennifer thought about it. He was right. She knew he was right.

"Just give me an hour or two, then," she said. "I can't help being the way I am. It just seems to me that my good news might be bad news for somebody else. I wonder if one of the Mennyms has died?"

Elsie Layton, Jennifer's mother, came to tea on the Saturday before Christmas. She sat in the taxi with an M & S bag on her knee and two others on the seat beside her. They were filled with presents for all the family.

"Sound the horn," she said to the driver. "Let them know I'm here."

Tom and Anna came to the door. Anna dashed forward, Tom following, and the two of them picked up the carrier bags which Elsie had stacked together on the icy pavement. By that time, Jennifer was at the open door ready to greet her mother.

And Elsie's first words to her daughter were, "So you've got the house at last! And not before time! But I must say, I don't know why you haven't been to collect the keys."

They went into the sitting room and sat down. Elsie noted once again her daughter's failures as a housewife, a room surface-tidy but with dust in the corners and too many books and other paraphernalia lying around.

"You could certainly *do* with more space," said Elsie.

"So you keep saying," said Jennifer, tight-lipped.

Lorna came along later in the afternoon with baby Matthew in his carry-cot. The baby was four months old and everybody's favorite. Albert brought them, but he did not stay. The whole clan gathering could be a bit overpowering.

"I'll come back for you about half-six," he said, and made his escape.

Everyone crowded round to admire the baby and persuade him to laugh, his one and only accomplishment so far. He chortled loudly till Elsie called them all to order saying, "Don't let him get too excited. He shouldn't be laughing like that at his age. It can't be good for him."

To change the subject, Lorna said, "So what do you think about the family moving to Brocklehurst Grove, Gran? It should be an interesting New Year."

"If I'd had anything to do with it, they would have moved in for Christmas," said Elsie. "They knew the house was theirs over a week ago. You'd think she'd at least have got the keys and had a look at the place."

Jennifer said nothing but her face took on a look of silent stubbornness that her mother recognized.

"I don't think even you could move a house in a couple of weeks, Gran," said Lorna, smiling at her grandmother. "But we could pop in and get the keys on Monday, Mum. The office should still be open then. Christmas Day's not till Wednesday.''

''No!'' said Jennifer sharply. ''I don't want to hear another word about those keys. I'll collect them in January and not before. There's plenty to do at Christmas without looking at houses.''

☙ 20 ❧

Number 5
Brocklehurst Grove

"And if you should need any information regarding the contents of the house, for example, you should contact Rothwell and Ramshaw. Their Mr. Dobb will be able to help you."

"Contents?" said Jennifer, looking doubtfully at Tom. She had been expecting to visit an empty house. The surveyor's report had mentioned the absence of rising damp, the sizes of the various rooms and the fact that the roof appeared to be sound. It had made no reference at all to contents.

"From what I gather," said Mr. Cromarty, looking down at a paper on his desk, "the Mennyms seem to have left a considerable amount of property behind them. It may, of course, have belonged to the original owner, Kate Penshaw, in which case they could have felt that the property went with the house. You will recall that they were formerly Miss Penshaw's paying guests. I'm afraid I can't tell you any more. Mr. Dobb will be the best person to ask."

As soon as they left the solicitor's office Jennifer began to work herself into a frenzy of worry.

"I wonder what he meant? What sort of property? If there's a lot of furniture in there, Tom, it will have to go. I don't care how old it is or how lovely it is, or anything—I can't live with other people's furniture."

"Nobody says you have to," said Tom. "If there's stuff there we don't want, we'll get rid of it."

The next day, a bitterly cold, wet Friday, Tom set off with Jennifer on the trip to Brocklehurst Grove. Anna came along with them. Lorna appeared just as they were setting out, having left Albert to look after Matthew. Ian was at work, Keith was still in bed, and Robert was somewhere in Germany. The winter holiday was not yet over.

Tom made a detour to another bit of suburbia to pick up Elsie. Jennifer moved into the backseat between Lorna and Anna so that her mother could sit in front. It was Elsie who directed Tom onto the road to Brocklehurst Grove. He did not need directions, but she gave them anyway.

"And now," she said, as they turned into the square, "we are here. Your new home!"

Jennifer looked up at the house, an imposing three-story building with a broad drive and a large front garden.

"It's big," she said.

"You knew that," said Elsie. "I've told you plenty of times."

Elsie was the only one of the family who had ever been inside Number 5, but that was a very long time ago.

They left the car out in the street, went through the wrought-iron gates and up to the front door. Even from the outside the house did not look empty. Eyes could be peeping from behind those net curtains, thought Jennifer with a shiver. She half-expected someone to come out and challenge them. Tom took the keys from his pocket and selected two that looked as if they would fit the locks. The front door opened and they all crowded in, anxious to escape the cold and damp.

Inside the hall, their first impression was that they were entering a home that was still lived in. They could feel the warmth, in cozy contrast with the bleak weather outside. There were carpets on the floor and up the staircase. A gate-legged table stood beneath a mirror on the wall.

"I feel like an intruder," said Jennifer as she looked at the closed doors around the hallway. To open them seemed like trespassing.

Her mother had no such qualms. "Let's press on," she said. "There's a lot to see and it will be dark soon."

Anna put her finger to the light switch and on came the light.

"They haven't had the electricity switched off!" Lorna exclaimed. "They should have seen to that before they left."

"Just as well, though," said Elsie. "It gives us a much better chance to look at things."

Jennifer said nothing.

They looked into the sitting room, the room the Mennyms always called the lounge, and were surprised to see that it was completely furnished in a mixture of styles that showed quite clearly that not all of the furniture could have belonged to Kate Penshaw. There was even a fairly modern television set. On various shelves there were books and ornaments. On top of a bureau there was a workbasket with threads and needles in it.

"This is spooky," said Anna, with a sly look at her mother. "It looks as if they haven't moved out at all."

"Don't be silly," said Tom. "They've definitely moved out. We have all the papers we need to prove it. When we've seen the whole house, I'll ring this Mr. Dobb and clear up any queries we might have. One thing at a time. And don't let's jump to any conclusions."

Jennifer opened the breakfast room door and spotted a mistake that Tulip had made. On the desk in the corner, a table lamp was still lit. Beside it was an old black telephone.

"I wonder if the phone's working," said Anna, following her mother into the room.

"Of course not," said Jennifer, but Anna picked up the receiver anyway and found that the line was buzzing.

"It is working, Mum, it is," she said. "Just listen."

Tom came into the room.

"It's a funny way to leave a house," he had to concede. "But we'll sort it out. I'll use that phone now and have a word with Mr. Dobb. He'll give us some answers."

Anna went on ahead to look at the rest of the house. She was the first to go upstairs. Lorna and her grandmother were in the day nursery. There were so many things to look at they hardly knew where to start.

"Mr. Dobb?" said Tom.

"Speaking. Can I help you?" said the voice at the other end of the line.

"I'm Tom Gladstone, Jennifer's husband. We are just looking round Number 5 Brocklehurst Grove. We were told that you would be able to answer any queries."

"Yes?" said the voice.

"You may not know this, but the electricity has not been turned off and the telephone hasn't been disconnected."

There was a pause while Mr. Dobb double-checked with the information in the Mennyms' letter.

"Ah, yes," he said, "that is quite in order. When you take over the utilities for the house, the accounts left over from the previous owner will be settled in full. Feel free to use them in the interim. You have been given explicit permission to do so."

"That was nice of them," said Tom as he put down the phone.

"But we'll not take advantage," said Jennifer. "We'll have the changeover made as soon as possible, whether we move in or not."

Elsie came into the breakfast room just in time to hear what they were saying.

"What do you mean?" she said. "Of course you'll be moving in. And quickly. There is no point in leaving the house empty."

"I only wish it *were* empty," said Jennifer. She felt totally bewildered. Her father, from whom she had inherited the fair, wispy hair and the pale blue eyes, would have understood. They had been so alike in many ways, but Jack Layton had died ten years ago. Her mother's understanding of her daughter went no further than to comment, from time to time, that Jennifer was just like her dad. And that was not intended as a compliment.

They went up the stairs. On the next floor they looked into the big front bedroom, the room that had belonged to Joshua and Vinetta. A dressing gown was hanging on the inside of the door. There were hairbrushes and combs on the dressing table.

"This is preposterous," said Jennifer. "I am beginning to feel like Goldilocks invading the home of the three bears. Let's go home now. I've seen more than enough for one day."

Anna was already on the top landing. She peeped into the bathroom but could see little in the growing darkness, just enough to identify the bath and the washbasin and to know that this was a room almost identical to the one she had already seen on the floor below. There was no light on this landing. Anna missed the switch which was located between the doors of the bathroom and the room now labeled DOLL ROOM. That was the door Anna came to next. In the gloom, she did not see the black letters on the polished wood. She turned the door handle, thinking to go in and switch on the light inside. The door creaked open till it was stopped by an obstruction. By now the room, east-facing and nearly into darkness, was all shades of gray.

Anna looked down to see why the door had ceased to open. She saw, with horror she saw, a woman's leg and foot, the drapery of a longish skirt. Anna jumped and, staring into the room, was instantly aware of shadowy figures, all seated slouched in crowded chairs, but completely motionless, still as death. She made no attempt to switch on the light. She turned and ran screaming down the stairs.

"Mum, Dad, Mum, Dad, Dad, Dad!" she yelled. "There's a room full of bodies. Dead bodies. Tons of them, all dead!"

❧ 21 ❧

Dead Bodies!

Anna ran to her mother's arms, shuddering and obviously terrified. Jennifer gave a wondering look at Tom. Dead bodies? *Dead bodies?* Without a word, Tom ran up the stairs, taking them two at a time. Anna, still clinging to her mother, yelled after him. "It's the room at the back, Dad, the one next to the bathroom."

For a chilling few moments that seemed to last forever they all stood and waited in breathless silence.

Then they heard Tom laugh, a faintly hysterical, relieved laugh. He had turned on the light in the doll room and seen the strange family of rag dolls.

"It's all right," he called. "They aren't dead people. They aren't people at all. They are just dolls. Come up and see them."

Anna, tugging her mother by the hand, led the way. Terror gave way to curiosity. Lorna and her grandmother followed. They all crowded into the doorway of the room full of dolls and what they saw filled them with amazement.

"What does it mean?" said Lorna. She gazed at the doll in the straight-backed carver chair, sitting there with its chin on its chest, its face a fine stocking-stitch, its eyes amber beads. The hair on its head was wiry and threaded with gray. Its arms were folded across its chest.

Elsie looked closely at the grandmother doll, a little old lady of a doll with silver hair and a blue-and-white checked pinny. The spectacles on the bridge of the fine little nose (stiffened with buckram, thought Elsie, very well made) had slipped askew. Elsie straightened them.

Cautiously, Anna approached the dolls on the settle. The mother doll's arms were stretched out round her children, but the boy had fallen sideways so that the upper half of his body dangled over the edge. Anna, growing brave, lifted him up and sat him so that he rested against the mother doll.

Elsie looked at Sir Magnus in his armchair. She sleeked back his hair with her hands and neatened the outline of his white mustache. Then she turned her attention to the doll in the bed, lying with arms outstretched over the counterpane, long red hair brushed smoothly onto her shoulders. The green glass eyes glittered where the light caught them. Dolls, clearly dolls, magnificent, with a wealth of detail that in some cases included eyelashes and fingernails, as well as lips so finely stitched they looked almost able to speak.

"They're wonderful," said Elsie. "Where on earth have they come from?"

It was Jennifer who first saw the note on the dressing table. It was in a very large, very conspicuous envelope. Only their wonder at the dolls had delayed them from seeing it earlier. Jennifer picked it up and read the inscription:

"I suppose we should open it," she said.

She looked at Tom. He took the envelope from her and tore it open. From it he took out a single sheet of paper, older-looking paper, written on in ink. He held it up and read it aloud.

" 'The dolls in this room,' " he read, " 'are my people. Work of my hands and of my heart. Please, love them.' And it is signed 'Kate Penshaw.' "

"That is beautiful," said Lorna, "and so are the dolls. Whatever we do, we must take care of them."

Elsie nodded.

Jennifer looked round the room with mounting horror. This was a totally unexpected situation. She was filled with an awareness of other people living their own lives with their own eccentricities in this house that might one day be her home.

"I can't," she said wildly. "I know the message is beautiful and I know the dolls are beautiful, but if loving them means keeping them in this house, I just can't do it."

She looked round at them, at the old man in the armchair, the girl in the bed, at the nanny nursing the baby, the children, their mother, the figure with its head on its chest that was clearly meant to be the father, and at the little old woman in the basket chair. They were not as realistic as dummies in shop windows, but somehow they were eerily real. Jennifer steeled herself to say what she felt she must say next.

"I can't live here," she said quietly, grasping the back of the one empty chair in the room. "I don't think I could ever live here."

Elsie gave her daughter a look of strong disapproval.

"Don't talk nonsense," she said. "Of course you can live here. The dolls will be easily disposed of, if they worry you so much. Good gracious, girl, the place is ready to move into. You could all move here tomorrow if you wanted to. You wouldn't even need to bring a teaspoon!"

"No!" said Jennifer vehemently. "Definitely no!"

Before Elsie could speak again, Tom intervened.

"Let's not start any arguments," he said. "We'll work something out. I think perhaps we really should go home now and think about it."

Elsie gave a sniff but said no more. Watched keenly by Anna, she went round all of the dolls, adjusting them in their seats. She scrutinized each one very minutely.

"They are very well made," she said. "If you don't want to keep them, you should offer them for sale. I am sure you would get a good price for them. I don't know how they would rate as antiques, but they can't be far short and they are so perfect some collector is sure to want them."

"Grandmother," said Lorna, outraged. "We can't possibly sell them. We may be able to sell everything else in the house if we want, but we can't sell the dolls. That would be a terrible thing to do. It would be going against the wishes of the dead. Look how wonderful the Mennyms were, keeping the dolls perfect all these years.

And they weren't even family! We have inherited a responsibility."

"Well, *we* can't keep them," said Jennifer. "Before we can give so much as a thought to living here, the dolls will have to go."

"I don't see why we can't just leave them in this room." said Lorna. "The house is big enough. You could lock the door and leave them there. You need never look at them again, if you don't want to. I wouldn't mind checking on them from time to time, dusting the room and making sure that they come to no harm."

"Keeping the dolls shut away in this room would hardly be a way of loving them," said Tom. "They've probably been on display somewhere. My guess is that the Mennyms simply stored them in this room when they were leaving."

"We could always try to sell them to someone who *would* love them," said Elsie, shrewd as ever.

"Not sell them—give them," said Lorna, suddenly inspired. "We must find someone who will love them and care for them, and we must give them away."

"Hold hard," said Tom. "Before we make any plans at all, I think I should have another word with Mr. Dobb. I don't suppose he'll be in the office now. It's rather late, and I don't want to use the phone here again. I'll ring him from home on Monday."

"And it's not just the dolls," said Jennifer. "It's everything. I don't want to live with other people's memories."

Poor Mennyms! They had been so thorough in their preparations, making sure that their finances were left in order, making sure that their cloth bodies should be seemly in death. But not one of them had given any thought to the impact a house full of *things* could have on a family of real, live people.

The oversight was strange, but understandable. The Mennyms had come to life in a fully furnished home. There had been clothes in the wardrobes, furniture and fittings all over the house. Kate Penshaw herself had never moved into an empty house. She had been born, and had lived all her life at Number 5 Brocklehurst Grove. Memories almost inexhaustible of things she had known and read and seen had been passed on to her creations and embellished by them over the years. Moving into an empty house was simply an area not one of them had ever explored. Appleby's imagination might have run to such lengths. but she was already dead.

❧ 22 ❧

A Problem to Solve

"**S**top it, all of you! I don't care how much the things in that house might be worth. I am not interested. All I know is that either those Mennyms were in terrible trouble when they left, or they are totally inconsiderate and too rich to care. Whatever the case, I want nothing at all to do with anything that has ever belonged to them. I certainly don't want to make a profit out of them. The house is mine. Only the house. And I don't want to see it again until it is completely empty."

Jennifer was furious. She had listened to the family going hammer-and-tongs over the contents of Number 5 Brocklehurst Grove for the past hour, and she had had enough.

"All right, Mother," said Lorna, "you've made your point. But those things are all yours. Mr. Dobb said they were—yours to dispose of as you think fit. None of us would want to make a profit out of Aunt Kate's dolls. To sell them would be a violation. But the rest of the stuff has no claim on your sympathy. Things are just things. And if they are worth money, you have a better right to that money than anybody else."

Jennifer sighed.

"Just at this moment," she said, "I would like nothing better than to call in some charity workers and ask *them* to clear the house, furniture, ornaments, pictures, carpets, the lot.''

"What about the dolls?" said Lorna. "We can't give them to just any old charity without knowing that they are going to be cared for. They were important to Aunt Kate, and she was family, and the house was originally hers."

"You feel so strongly about it," said Jennifer, "you see to it. You'd certainly make a better job of it than I would."

Lorna looked at her mother sharply. Was she being sarcastic? But no, not entirely. There was obviously a measure of sarcasm in her words, but it did not contradict her meaning. She really would be just as pleased to let Lorna take the reins. It was something Tom had thought possible when they discussed it the night before.

"If Lorna wants to take over, let her. She'll know what she's doing. And she's very concerned to do the right thing."

"Would you not rather . . . ?" began Jennifer.

"If necessary, I'll see to things, but on the whole, I think I'd prefer not to. We don't want your mother saying I am taking too keen an interest in the family fortune. That house is *yours,* not mine."

"What's mine is yours, Tom Gladstone, and you should know that by now."

It was eventually settled that Lorna and Albert should take on the task of finding a good home for the dolls and then emptying the house of all its other contents.

"I won't tell you what to do with anything," said

Jennifer. "All I ask is that you don't discuss it with me, or in front of me. I don't want to hear anything else about that house until it is completely empty. There's no hurry. And whatever you do will be right by me."

"In the meantime," said Tom, "I think we should put this house up for sale. Then we'll have cash to spare for new furniture when the time comes."

Jennifer was more than pleased to pass on the responsibility to the others.

"I'll look after Matthew any time," she said. "If you have anything to see to, just bring him to me. That's what grannies are for!"

The word *granny* reminded Jennifer that there was another grandmother to be considered. Elsie must not be ignored. And Jennifer remembered how pleased she herself had been when Albert gave her the jug from Comus House. The only value Jennifer could recognize in objects was the sentimental one.

"There is just one thing," said Jennifer. "Your grandmother might want some keepsake from Brocklehurst Grove. She did visit there when she was very young. Let her choose anything she would like."

So it came about that Albert Pond returned to Number 5 Brocklehurst Grove. He entered the street and did not recognize anything about it. He looked up at the statue of Matthew James Brocklehurst and had no memory of ever having noticed it before. Nothing about Number 5 gave any signals. Albert suffered no sense of déjà-vu. It was a house that had once been the home of a family called Mennym and that now belonged to his mother-in-law. That was all.

He and Lorna went in at the front door, and at that point they both had the feeling that the spirit of the place hung heavy in the air.

"It is rather spooky," said Lorna.

"That's because of the furniture," said Albert. "It is full of other people's memories, or so we believe. It is all a matter of imagination really. Jennifer has it to an extreme. But we all have it to some degree. It'd be strange if we didn't."

Lorna was anxious to show Albert the dolls.

"We can look at the rest of the house later," she said. "But first you must see Kate's People."

Albert smiled. They went up the two flights of stairs to the top landing. The stair carpet was vaguely familiar, but then stair carpet always is. Lorna led the way to the Doll Room.

"There," she said, as they went inside, "what do you think of them?"

Albert looked round at the dolls wonderingly. They were all nicely seated now, not lurched to this side or that. Elsie and Anna had arranged them well. Looked at myopically, they could almost be real people. Kate's People was what they would always be now, for every member of the Gladstone family, and for whoever their new owner might be. Though "owner" seemed an odd word. Perhaps "keeper" would be better, like the keeper of a motor car. Or, better still, "guardian."

Albert looked at each doll in turn.

"They're portraits," he said as he looked at Sir Magnus. "They have to be."

"Portraits?" said Lorna.

"Likenesses," said Albert, "probably based upon

Kate's own family, or maybe on her lodgers. That would account for the Mennyms being so concerned about them."

"They weren't concerned enough to take them along with them," said Lorna.

Albert was looking at Vinetta, seated between Poopie and Wimpey, with one arm round each of them.

"Maybe the Mennyms thought the dolls belonged here—if not in this house, then at least in this country. They might have returned to Denmark, for all we know," said Albert. "There's no use speculating. We'll never be sure of anything."

Then he turned at last and looked full in the face of Pilbeam. An inexplicable shock went through him, a turmoil of feelings, the uppermost he wrongly identified as pity. Like Lancelot looking on the Lady of Shalott, he felt called upon to say how beautiful she was.

"She could be modeled on an ancestor of yours," he said, looking over his shoulder at Lorna. One hand rested gently on Pilbeam's arm. "She has your coloring."

"I don't think so," said Lorna. "I take after the Gladstones. That's not Kate's side of the family. I don't suppose she ever knew any of them."

Then she laughed at herself. For one brief moment she had felt jealous, jealous of an old cloth doll!

"We'd better go now," she said. "I'll have to get Matthew home to bed. We'll come again later in the week. It is a problem, but we'll find a solution somehow. But now that you've seen them, Albert, you have to agree that Aunt Kate's wishes must be honored. A home for her people—that's the job we've taken on. And we have to do it properly.''

Albert smiled nervously. Marriage had given him more self-assurance, but he still had moments when he wished devoutly for a quiet life.

❧ 23 ❧

Greater Dolls

Lorna went to Heatherton Hall.

She had rung up beforehand and requested an interview with the director of the Theme Museum without knowing exactly what the "theme" was. Heatherton Hall was a new museum in an old building. It was built in Palladian style, very formal, very eighteenth century, set well back from the highway in a wooded park. Lorna found its telephone number in the Yellow Pages and, since it was just five miles north of Castledean, she thought it would be a good place to try. A theme museum—might it not welcome a family of rag dolls?

"Miss Summerbell will see you at nine-thirty on Tuesday, if that is all right with you. She can give you half an hour before the gallery opens," said the young man on the other end of the line after he had consulted the lady her subordinates privately called Minerva, after the armour-clad goddess of wisdom.

"Thank you," said Lorna. "I'll be there."

At nine-twenty-five, Lorna drove into the huge carriageway that led up to the mansion. It was an icy cold day, but dazzlingly bright. She stopped the car at the wall beneath two massive stone staircases that led up from each side of the façade to a palatial front entrance.

Suddenly Lorna, usually so self-possessed, began to feel shy. What was she going to say to the director?

She restarted the car and drove round the side of the house following the sign that said VISITORS' CAR PARK. Nothing venture, she thought later as she pushed open the heavy glass door.

"I'm afraid the galleries are not open yet. There *is* a notice on the door outside," said one of the girls behind the desk in the entrance hall.

"I've come to see the director," said Lorna.

"Do you have an appointment?" said the girl, glancing down at the book on the desk.

"Yes," said Lorna. "My name's Lorna Pond. I rang up two days ago."

"Take a seat," said the girl, gesturing toward a long wooden form fixed to the far wall. "I'll be with you in a minute."

The minute was at least five, and felt like twenty-five.

When the girl came back she was followed by a young man who came toward Lorna, hand outstretched in greeting.

"Mrs. Pond," he said. "We spoke on the telephone. My name is Andrew. Miss Summerbell won't be free for another ten minutes or so, but she's asked me to show you a little of the gallery, if you like. We'll have time to see some of the exhibits on the ground floor."

"Thank you," said Lorna. "That should be interesting."

They went through a set of double doors into a corridor paneled with large panes of glass. Behind each wall of glass was a room, fully furnished and apparently lived in.

The first room had the name JANE AUSTEN inscribed in discreet little letters on a metal plaque fixed to the center base of the glass frame. Through it, Lorna saw the Pump Room at Bath. It was an exact replica—the long windows, the columned walls and the high-arched apse where stood the great clock. Gentlemen in frock coats and ladies in high-waisted dresses were in the act of walking up and down, or sitting cosily by each other to observe the company. These were all dolls, of course, but such dolls! One almost expected them to resume walking and talking at any minute.

The next room was occupied by Forsytes, sitting round the drawing room at Timothy's place in the Bayswater Road. All eleven chairs were there, and the sofa, the tables, the cabinet, and even the grand piano. Most of the seats were occupied. The dolls that sat very upright on them were well-dressed, wealthy Victorian ladies and gentlemen, all looking conscious of their own importance. And every doll appeared to be on the point of relaying some juicy bit of gossip. Galsworthy would have smiled to see them.

In the third room sat Sherlock Holmes, the bowl of his pipe tucked in his right hand, looking from hooded eyes at a mysterious lady visitor. His friend, Dr. Watson, stood with one arm stretched up to rest on the ornate mantelpiece above the handsome fireplace. The room was complete with pictures, books, ornaments and all the carved and decorated furniture of the period. The woman was deeply distressed, holding to her eyes a lace-edged handkerchief. Holmes was just about to speak. . . .

Lorna followed her guide without a word. Andrew gave her a commentary as they went.

At the end of this corridor they came to the strangest room of all. It was well lit, but draped all in black, its only occupant being a very large mirror, framed with a narrow band of ebony. Lorna could not help but see herself in it, her outdoor clothes looking bulky and incongruous.

"This room, as you see, is labeled FIN DE SIÈCLE," said Andrew, looking rather sheepish, feeling the need to explain something that he clearly regarded as peculiar. "That means 'end of the century.' Miss Summerbell sees it as symbolic. It speaks of our aridity, dryness, lack of inspiration."

His smile showed that he was conscious of speaking in quotation marks. In a more comfortable voice he added, "I like the mirror though. If we look at the contemporary world, we are bound to see ourselves."

Lorna looked at the room and tried to imagine it filled with furniture from Brocklehurst Grove, and with Kate's People seeming to live in it. At once she felt sorry for the rag dolls, and for their long-dead maker. Wonderful they might be, but in a place like this they would stand out as the work of a gifted amateur. Lorna felt increasingly embarrassed.

"I'm afraid there's not time to show you more," said Andrew, looking at his watch. "Miss Summerbell will be ready to see you now."

Then he led the way back to the entrance hall. Lorna had just time to notice, briefly, an "interior" to the other side of the FIN DE SIÈCLE room that was really an "exterior" depicting Mr. Pickwick and his friends departing from Dingley Dell on a frosty morning, ready to go skating, old Wardle leading the way and poor Mr. Winkle looking "exquisitely uncomfortable." The next window showed the parlor at Haworth Parsonage with the sisters seated around the table, Emily deeply engrossed in her own writing, Charlotte leaning toward Anne to show her something in a book she is holding. At any moment, it seemed, the fingers would turn the page.

A room labeled E. M. FORSTER was still being prepared, signs of a courtroom in an Indian city, dust covers on various boxes and pieces of furniture, but no figures yet. The room next to it was not even labeled, but long ladders and cloth covers showed that it too was being made ready for an exhibit.

From the wide corridor, Andrew led Lorna into a narrow passage, along to a room with DIRECTOR written in large gold letters on a beveled glass door. He tapped at the door.

"Come in," said a contralto voice.

"You can go in," said Andrew, holding the door ajar for her. He almost felt like warning her about the overpowering lady she was about to meet, but that would have been a breach of loyalty.

"Good morning, Mrs. Pond," said Miss Summerbell as Lorna entered. "I'm sorry I had to keep you waiting. Do take a seat."

Lorna sat down on the low chair placed strategically a few yards away from a large and very solid desk. The chair was so low that she was obliged to look up at the very large and solid director seated on the throne behind it. Lorna recognized the technique, and was more amused than impressed. But she *was* uneasy neverthe-less. It was impossible not to be impressed by the Theme Museum's lifelike array of dolls.

"I believe you have a proposition to make," said Miss Summerbell, looking very earnestly down at her visitor, as if taking her seriously was paying a compli-ment.

Before Lorna could open her mouth, Miss Sum-merbell gave a sweep of the hand, and went on, "I think I should warn you, before you begin, that I see people week after week making suggestions for creating a display in the FIN DE SIÈCLE. They fail to see that the room is already complete. It is not even as if there were no other rooms for which they could make suggestions. My FIN DE SIÈCLE salon seems to make people very un-easy! So if—"

It was Lorna's turn to interrupt. Embarrassed she might be, but by the situation she'd got herself into, not by the disdainful manner of the museum's self-important director.

"Nothing of the kind," said Lorna coldly. "I had not even seen that room until today. But now that I have seen it, and the rest of the exhibits in there, I feel I owe you an apology for wasting your time. I had some dolls to offer you, life-sized dolls, but they would not fit in here."

Miss Summerbell's eyes gleamed. She was not about to throw away a donation without knowing what it was. The museum space was by no means full yet. She leaned across the desk and in a much more intimate voice said, "Let me be the judge, Mrs. Pond. Tell me about your dolls. Why do you think they wouldn't fit?"

"They are rag dolls, not models," said Lorna. "If this were a handicraft museum, they might have a place here."

Miss Summerbell looked intrigued.

"You have seen only one wing of the first floor, I believe," she said. "Even that is still in process of being completed. There are other floors. This is a new museum. There will be other themes. How did you come by the rag dolls? Provenance is important."

"They were made over half a century ago by a member of my family," said Lorna.

"I think perhaps I should at least see them," said Miss Summerbell. "You really do want to part with them?"

Lorna was taken off guard and said simply, "Yes. We do."

"There are certain conditions," said Miss Summerbell, becoming businesslike. "We cannot pay for them. We are not allowed to offer money for any outside contributions—"

"It's not like that," said Lorna quickly, and she was about to explain that her mind was made up that this museum would not be right for Kate's People. It was too grand a place by far. But Miss Summerbell ignored her. For anyone to interrupt the director of Heatherton Hall was very unusual. This young woman had already dared to make one interruption. She could not be permitted to make another. Miss Summerbell went on speaking as if Lorna had never opened her mouth.

"—and if you donate them you relinquish all rights to them forever. They may be displayed, or stored. We are not allowed to sell them, but if they are not suitable for this museum, they can be passed on to another. And if they become infested in any way, or too damaged to repair, we have the right to dispose of them.''

Lorna looked horrified. No longer was she embarrassed. She stood up and said, "These dolls are Kate's People. They need someone to care for them, to cherish them, to love them. If you saw them, you would know that they have been loved and cherished for years and years. I couldn't possibly agree to those conditions, even if I wanted to.''

❦ 24 ❦

Consulting Mr. Dobb

Lorna sat on the bed in Poopie's room and held the Action Man in her hands. It was Hector, Poopie's old favorite, dressed in combat suit and bearing scars of battle on his rugged face. The door of the largest toy cupboard was wide open. Inside, neatly arranged on the shelves, just as Poopie had left them, were boxes of soldiers and Lego bricks and all sorts of equipment calculated to make a boy's life enjoyable. On the cupboard floor was a ship made out of Lego bricks, so detailed that the child who made it must have had enormous patience and tremendous skill.

Lorna had opened the cupboard door in her random prowling round the house. This was their second visit. The problem of the dolls was nowhere nearer being solved, but Lorna had decided that they should look at the other things in the house and consider what should be done with them.

The toy cupboard struck a chord that nothing else in the house had touched. A little boy had lived in this room and all of his treasures were stashed away there. Why had they been left behind? Was the child dead? His toys neatly tidied away by parents too sad to look at them again? And to the young mother, the thought of a child dying was heartbreaking. She was near to tears.

"Is something wrong?" said Albert, coming into the room.

Lorna looked up at him with a woebegone face.

"I think there is," she said. "I just opened that cupboard—and look what's in it. A boy's toys—soldier dolls, building bricks, all sort of things."

Albert sat on the bed beside her. He took the toy soldier from her and looked at it, musing.

"It does seem strange," he said. "I was just coming to tell you about my find. *All* of the cupboards and wardrobes in this house seem to be full. The Mennyms certainly didn't pack for their journey."

Albert's words set Lorna thinking. Sorrow changed to foreboding. Where were the Mennyms? What could have happened to them? She looked at Albert, waiting for him to share her suspicions.

"Nobody," she said slowly, "absolutely nobody, goes away and leaves *all* of their personal possessions behind them. We'll have to do something about it. I think we should inform the police."

Albert thought of Jennifer, and of how nervous his mother-in-law was about anything suspicious or eerie.

"Your mother will be upset," he said. "I was hoping we would be able to clear everything out without her knowing."

"She needn't know," said Lorna. "We won't tell her."

Albert looked at Lorna incredulously.

"Impossible," he said. "Think of it logically. If there is any real need to call in the police, goodness knows what secrets this house might be hiding. We would have to keep your mother informed. We couldn't just leave her in the dark.''

Lorna sighed.

''Well, what do *you* think we should do then?'' she said.

Albert thought hard before answering.

''I think we should go to the offices of Rothwell and Ramshaw and have a long chat with their Mr. Dobb. He should be able to shed some light on all this if anybody can.''

Albert and Lorna were shown into the senior clerk's office, a room lacking in privacy because small windows stretching the length of one wall looked out onto the reception area.

''Do sit down, Mr. Pond, Mrs. Pond,'' said Mr. Dobb, raising himself almost to standing position before collapsing again into his leather chair. He was very fat, and looked well past the normal age of retirement.

''Now,'' he said, ''how can I help you?''

Albert let Lorna do the talking. It saved the two of them talking at once! She explained the problem while Mr. Dobb nodded and listened.

''So,'' she finished, ''what we are really concerned about is whether there could have been any sort of foul play.''

Mr. Dobb looked down at the Mennym file; more particularly, he looked at the third page of Tulip's closely written letter.

''Well, Mrs. Pond,'' he began, ''I think I will be able to give you some reassurance on that point. It is clear from the Mennyms' letter that they decided, as a family, to leave everything behind them. It was, I fancy, a symbolic gesture. There is, you must surely think, something quite noble about it. They go out in the clothes they stand up in. They close the door behind them and they venture forth to start a new life.''

"Is that what it says there?" said Lorna, leaning forward and trying to see what was written on the sheet of paper in Mr. Dobb's hand.

Mr. Dobb placed the paper firmly in the file.

"My client's instructions are confidential, Mrs. Pond," he said severely. "I cannot possibly divulge all their business. You may know whatever you need to know. And I tell you now that there is nothing in the least bit shady about the property the Mennyms left in Brocklehurst Grove. You may keep anything you wish. You may sell anything that is of no use to you. It is an unusual arrangement, I grant you, but it is perfectly legal. Is there anything else I can tell you?"

Lorna looked furious. Albert put one hand out to restrain her.

"I know now how my mother felt," she said, thrusting Albert's hand away. "I know why she was so cross with the Mennyms. Noble? Is it noble to leave so many bits and pieces to be gathered up by perfect strangers? We hardly know where to start."

Mr. Dobb puffed out a sigh. Why do people have to make everything so complicated?

"There are all sorts of ways of emptying a house," he said. "If it is a real trouble to you, I can make arrangements for the premises to be cleared. It will be extra work for me, but that will be chargeable to the Mennym account."

"The Mennym account?" said Albert.

"Yes," said Mr. Dobb, turning thankfully toward him. Men, Mr. Dobb thought, are so much more reasonable than women. "Everything to do with the departure of the Mennyms is to be wound up by this firm. They have made ingenious arrangements to pay all expenses incurred, including, I may say, the cost of this interview. You will not be sent a bill. Perhaps you and your wife should talk it over, Mr. Pond, and then you can let me know what you wish us to do."

Lorna clenched her fists. She stood up abruptly.

"We'll be going now," she said. "We know all we need to know. We shall not be troubling you again."

"No trouble, Mrs. Pond, no trouble at all," said Mr. Dobb, half-rising.

"We'll just have to accept what we've been told," said Albert. "So we find a home for the dolls and we look for a dealer to take everything else off our hands."

"We'll be robbed, if we aren't careful," said Lorna. "There must be some way of getting an honest valuation and selling things properly."

Albert and Lorna were sitting in the little living room at Calder Park. Matthew was asleep in his cot upstairs. It was the day after their encounter with Mr. Dobb. They had talked and talked about what to do and how and when.

"What happened when you sold Comus House?" asked Lorna.

"An agent sold the house," he said, "and I had someone come from London to value the contents."

"That's what I mean," said Lorna eagerly. "That is what *we* should do."

"I don't think so," said Albert. "It was a waste of time and effort. To be perfectly honest, it was embarrassing. People think because things are old they are worth a lot. I suppose they might be sometimes. But more often than not they are just nineteenth-century junk. Five hundred years from now they might be interesting as artifacts."

"Even so . . ." began Lorna.

"Even so," said Albert, "it is not what your mother wants. We are not looking to make a profit. Our job is simply to empty the house ready for your family to move in. And in case you haven't noticed, most of the furniture there is not even all that old."

"So where do we start?" said Lorna.

"We start by having a proper look at everything in the house and making some sort of list so that we can give anyone interested an idea of what they will be coming to see."

"What about the dolls?" said Lorna.

Albert gave her a helpless look.

"I suppose," he said, "we're just stuck waiting for inspiration."

❧ 25 ❧

A Sunday Survey

On Sunday morning after church, the Ponds resolved to make another assault on the Mennym mountain. They drove to Rimstead to leave Matthew with his grandparents.

"We'll make a proper inventory this time," said Lorna. "It's about time we got organized. We'll go through each room in turn and list the contents under four headings—large furniture, small furniture, clothing and miscellaneous. The miscellaneous will include pictures, ornaments, and any other items not included in the other lists."

Lorna the librarian was about to be in her element. She had brought two clipboards, one blue, one red, and several pens, also in a variety of colors.

When they arrived at Elmtree Road, they were asked to stay for lunch—a feast which usually occurred late afternoon—but Lorna was adamant about their need to go soon and get on with the work. Jennifer was in the kitchen. Tom said, "Well, at least sit down and have a cup of tea. How are things going?"

He gave a cautious look toward the door. The do-not-mention-it-in-front-of-me dictum still held good. Jennifer often portrayed herself as being a weakling crushed by the strength of all her family, but when she was stubborn, she was stubborn! The occasions were rare, but all the more respected for that.

"Things aren't going at all," said Albert.

"That's not exactly true," said Lorna. "Gran came and took away some of the things she fancied. It took two trips to and from her house."

Tom looked amused.

"What did she take, for goodness sake?"

"A couple of hideous basket chairs with high backs, a lot of small ornaments and the biggest picture in the house. You might have noticed it. It was hanging above the fireplace in the sitting room," said Lorna.

"I rather liked that picture," said Albert. "It reminded me of the view from Comus House."

"And that's all you've managed to get rid of?" said Tom.

"That's all so far," said Lorna. "But we are going there today to make a full inventory of the contents, and we are going to be really businesslike about disposing of them."

"What about the dolls?" said Tom.

"I have a few other museums I mean to try—folk museums, that sort of thing. Heatherton Hall was a mistake, but no one can say I don't learn."

Albert and Lorna reached Number 5 Brocklehurst Grove shortly after two o'clock. They went in the door that was by now familiar, made their way to the kitchen, and sat down at the table, just as Joshua and Vinetta had so often done.

"Now," said Lorna, "you must take the blue clipboard and list all of the small furniture and the clothing. I'll do the large furniture and the miscellaneous. Small furniture is anything that can normally be moved from place to place by one person. So you count the chairs and small tables, etcetera. Do a fresh sheet for each room. I'll start on the ground floor and work my way up. You can start on the top floor and work your way down. That will make it less confusing.''

Albert took the blue clipboard from his wife's hands, smiled slightly and felt confused.

"Shall we have a cup of tea before we start?'' he said.

The brown teapot was still there and all the cups and saucers. Gas and electricity had already been signed over to the Gladstones. Lorna herself had brought emergency rations. But . . .

"No,'' she said. "We must get started straightaway. I don't want to waste any more time. Do you realize, it's nearly the end of January? We've spent three weeks getting nowhere.''

"That's not what you said to your father,'' said Albert.

"I was trying to be reassuring,'' said Lorna, looking dignified. "Dad has enough to worry about—getting Elmtree Road ready for selling.''

So they began the task of listing everything. Albert did not question why everything needed to be listed so precisely, though it was not at all what he had had in mind when he mentioned "some sort of list.'' But for Lorna, making lists was second nature, her way of dealing with anything and everything.

Suddenly, Albert called from the top floor.

"Come here a minute, Lorna. You must see this," he said.

Lorna, clipboard under her arm, went to the foot of the stairs.

"That's not the way we do it," she shouted up the stairs. "If you ask me to come and see things every few minutes we'll never get anywhere. List first, talk later."

"Come up here," said Albert emphatically. "I want you to see this now."

Lorna sighed and ran up the stairs.

"Well?" she said, following Albert into the big front bedroom. "What's so urgent?"

Albert took her to the wardrobe.

"What do you think of that?"

He pointed to the uniform, Sir Magnus Mennym's brilliant white naval uniform with its gold braid and epaulettes.

"Dazzling?" said Albert as he held one sleeve out for her closer inspection.

Lorna looked at the uniform more closely.

"It's not for real," she said. "It can't be. He'd have to be Admiral of the Fleet to wear something like that."

A look at all the other things in that wardrobe confirmed a suspicion that these things were fancy dress. A Noel Coward smoking jacket. A dressing gown in rich brocade with an ermine collar. Albert took it from its hanger and held it up for Lorna to see.

"The Tsar of Russia," he said as he draped it round his own shoulders.

"At the very least," said Lorna with a giggle. "Aren't they gorgeous?"

The clipboards were temporarily forgotten, but it was not time wasted. Seeing these fantastic clothes jogged Albert's memory. They reminded him of a shop down by the river, a very odd and very special shop.

"I think I know where to get rid of these," he said. "Waggons!"

"Waggons?"

"It's a sort of antique shop, down North Shore Road. I used to pass it years ago when my father took me to the office on the quayside. It was a jumble of all sorts, as I remember, but it specialized in theatrical costumes."

"It might not be there any more," Lorna pointed out.

"It might not," said Albert, "but it's the next place to try."

"Your turn?" said Lorna with a smile.

"My turn," said Albert. "I'll go down there one day next week."

❧ 26 ❧

Lesser Dolls

The shop was still there. And, what is more, it was exactly as Albert remembered it.

It was Saturday morning and he had just left his car at the Castledean Car Center for servicing. It was the first chance he'd had to look for the shop on North Shore Road. He walked alone down the long, curving street that led to the river. Either side were tall, stately buildings that now housed a multitude of offices. Across the bottom of this street was a huge, high-arched railway viaduct. And after that point came a jumbled mixture of buildings with dates that differed by as much as two hundred years, perhaps more. Shabby Victorian tenements rubbed shoulders with buildings that were standing when Charles the First was king. Albert made his way down and down till he came to where the North Shore Road skirted the river.

He turned right, walked a few yards and arrived at the shop he was seeking even sooner than he expected. It was double-fronted with old style windows that did not go right to the ground. The building above it was three stories high. The brickwork was sooty and the paintwork was drab. A sign across the shop front read L & P WAGGONS.

The sign had once been yellow edged with black, but now both colors were nearer to gray. The shop windows, however, were very clean and the displays inside them were orderly. In the window to the left there were well-polished tables and hat stands and small chests of drawers. In the right-hand window there was a rail curving backward in a half-moon shape and full of all sorts of clothing on hangers. In the center space was a theatrical chest with the lid thrown open and a couple of bright ball gowns artistically spilling out.

What made this shop memorably different from any other secondhand dealer was not the wares on display. It was the dolls.

At the far left-hand side of the left-hand window, the full-sized figure of a lady was seated at an old-fashioned treadle sewing machine. Her sister was at the far right-hand side of the right-hand window seated at a desk with her spindly fingers resting on the keys of an ancient typewriter. To mistake the two for real people one would, at the very least, have to be on a boat in the middle of the river. They were dressed as Victorian ladies in dark high-necked dresses trimmed with cream lace. On their heads were little cream lace caps surmounting wooden, yes wooden, buns. They were wooden betty dolls! *Huge* wooden betty dolls with brown wood faces and skeletal wooden hands. Their cheeks were painted bright red, their lips cupid-bowed, and their eyes, flat as fried eggs, had long black lashes sketched in thick lacquer above and below. They had fascinated Albert when he'd seen them years ago. And there they still were.

The shop door had a polished brass sneck with a

well-thumbed lip. It rattled as Albert pressed it down and as the door opened a cracked bell over the entrance gave out a jarring sound. The inside of the shop was as neat as the window. Every old and not-so-old piece of furniture was free from dust. There was no shop counter, but the owner was seated at an octagonal table pushed up against the left side wall. On the table were a number of filing cases, one of which had its drawer open. The owner looked up from her work when Albert came in.

"Hello," she said. "Can I help you?"

She was a woman in her sixties with wiry gray hair and a broad, flat-cheeked face. Her eyes were deep-set and very dark. Seated, she looked as if she would be a very big woman—broad shoulders, large, plump hands. It came as a shock when she stood up and Albert saw that she was the height of a child, no more than four-foot-six. As she came to meet him, her stumpy legs swung stiffly from the hip in a manner that looked painful. She was wearing a dark blue dress that reached nearly to her ankles, thick stockings, and a pair of heavy brown brogues.

"I don't know whether you can help or not," said Albert, looking worried. "I have some property to dispose of. It's very complicated."

"Well, come in and sit down," said the woman. "I'm not one for standing about, as you can see."

She smiled. Her expression was both friendly and confident. No one, but no one, would ever have to feel sorry for Daisy Maughan. In that instant, Albert knew that this woman was strong, reliable and almost heaven-sent. She looked like one who could solve problems.

"Well, Miss Waggons," he began.

Daisy laughed.

"I can't tell you how many times I've been called that. But it's not my name. I'm Daisy Maughan. But everybody calls me Daisy."

"So who are L. and P. Waggons?" asked Albert.

"Haven't the faintest idea," said Daisy. "My dad took over this shop seventy years ago. The owners before that were called Hirschman, and before that, way back in the last century, it was the Jacksons. But I have my own theory."

"Yes?" said Albert.

Daisy stood up again, taking the stick this time to make walking easier. She went to the front window. Albert followed. Daisy pointed to the wooden betty doll seated at the sewing machine.

"She's been here since long before my time. I call her Lily Waggons. And her over there," she added pointing with her stick to the other doll, "she's Polly Waggons."

Albert smiled and they went back to the octagonal table again.

"I think of them as family," said Daisy. "I do get lonely at times, especially since my sister Ada died. You should have seen Ada. She was such a tall woman, and thin as a reed."

"I'm sorry . . ." Albert began.

"No need for pity," said Daisy. "The secret is to accept everything. Loneliness is in some ways a privilege. Making the best of it is what counts. Saying good morning to Lily Waggons as I dust her sewing machine. Having a word with Polly about her typewriter."

"They're not for sale, I take it," said Albert.

"I should think not," said Daisy. "They were here when I was born. They'll be here when I die."

"Then what?" said Albert.

Daisy laughed again.

"I'm good for a few years yet," she said. "Before my time comes I'll find someone to take them over. I owe it to them. Now, let's get down to business. Or would you like a cup of tea first?"

"Business will be fine," said Albert. "We can have tea some other time."

Albert told Daisy all about the clothes and the furniture at Number 5 Brocklehurst Grove. She was a good listener. He ended up telling her everything, even the story of Kate's People and the doll room.

"I'd like to see this house," said Daisy when he paused. "I'm sure we'll be able to sort something out. When would you like me to come?"

"When would you be able to manage? I could probably come and take you there," said Albert. "I've just brought my car in for a service, but I should have it back on Monday."

"No need," said Daisy. "I'm quite happy coming by taxi. It's my one luxury. I go everywhere by taxi. Here in the morning, home at night. I even have a regular driver who fetches me most days, if he's at work."

"You don't live here then?" said Albert.

"Haven't lived here for forty-odd years," said Daisy. "I was born in the flat upstairs, but that's just a warren of stockrooms now. We thought about letting it but that would have been more bother than it was worth. And, when all came to all, Dad found the space useful for storage. The business was much bigger in his day. Mine is smaller, but more selective.''

She smiled as she remembered all the bric-a-brac and downright rubbish that had once filled most of the flat upstairs. It was a very large flat, on two floors, but it had suffered years of neglect.

''It was my mother that insisted on moving,'' she went on. ''There were no mod cons, absolutely none. The lavatory was outside in the yard. We used to bathe in a zinc bath and the water had to be heated in the fire boiler. Still, I do miss it sometimes at night. I used to love looking out of my window and seeing the lights on the river. I'd be there long after Mother thought I was fast asleep.''

She paused a moment to dwell on times gone by. Then she said briskly, ''So when do I come?''

''The sooner the better,'' said Albert.

''Wednesday afternoon do?'' said Daisy. ''I'm closed on Wednesday from twelve o'clock.''

''That'll be fine,'' said Albert. He too was ''closed on Wednesday day from twelve o'clock.'' It was a nice gap in his timetable. ''Lorna and I will be waiting for you.''

As he left, he looked once more at the wooden betty dolls. They were not as lifelike, or as finely made, as the rag dolls awaiting him at Brocklehurst Grove. But they were obviously loved.

✣ 27 ✣

Daisy

"**Y**ou shouldn't have told her everything," said Lorna. "She's a total stranger. What will she think of us?"

"It doesn't matter," said Albert. "She's a little old woman, very plump, very plain and slightly crippled. But I am telling you now, Lorna, there is something special about her. Don't ask me what it is. I don't know. But you'll see what I mean when you meet her."

Lorna looked at her watch. It was half-past one. She and Albert were sitting by the window in the sitting room at Number 5 Brocklehurst Grove waiting for Daisy's taxi to arrive. Their clipboards lay on the table, lists all neatly completed.

A few minutes later a car drew up in the street. The driver got out, went to the passenger door, helped Daisy out onto the pavement and escorted her through the front gate.

"You'll be all right now?" he said, making sure she was firm on her feet with her stout stick supporting her.

"Yes, Mike," she said. "I can manage from here, thanks. I'll give you a ring when I'm ready to go home. I don't expect I'll be more than an hour."

She walked up the path to the front door. She didn't need to knock. By the time she got there the door was already open and Albert and Lorna were waiting to take her inside.

"This is Lorna," said Albert, "Jennifer's daughter."

"And your wife," said Daisy with a smile. "I'm pleased to meet you, dear. I hope I can be of some help."

Lorna perceived something of the magic Albert had been trying to explain. It was as if an inner Daisy shone out, a Daisy who was inferior to no one. Here was a woman who could take control and make everything come right. There was no reason for believing this other than the look in her eye and the warmth in her voice.

"Where do you want me to start?" she said, coming straight to the point in a very reassuring way.

"I thought we could do a tour of the whole house, room by room, looking in all the cupboards as we go," said Lorna. "We have already listed the contents of each room, so that should make it easier."

"Unless you have some other ideas?" said Albert hastily.

"Not really," said Daisy, "but, if you don't mind, I would like to do the top floor first. That will get the going upstairs bit over with before I feel too tired. You two go on ahead of me. I'll follow nice and slowly."

"Are you sure?" said Lorna. "Perhaps we could give you a hand."

"No," said Daisy. "I can cope with all my disabilities. I've accepted my limitations and learned to live with them. That is a kind of happiness. Now go along up those stairs. I'll see you when I get there!"

She was almost laughing at herself as if being slow were some sort of a good joke.

Albert led the way up the stairs and Lorna followed. They walked quite slowly and were careful to include their visitor in their conversation.

"My mother wants rid of the carpets too," said Lorna over her shoulder. "I think she's carrying it all rather too far, but she is adamant."

"That's all right," said Daisy. "The carpets will be no problem."

When they reached the top landing, Albert went first into the big front bedroom where the uniform and all the other glories still hung in the wardrobe. Lorna was carrying the clipboards. She found the right sheet, read down the list and checked off each item. Daisy kept nodding thoughtfully and saying "mhmm" and "uhuu" under her breath. That room finished, they came out onto the landing. The room facing them was clearly labeled DOLL ROOM.

"That one next," said Daisy. "I'm looking forward to seeing those dolls."

They went in. Daisy went round the room and looked at each doll in turn. It was like royalty visiting the sick. She patted Joshua on the shoulder. She lingered over Pilbeam. She picked up Wimpey's doll and placed it in her arms. Poopie's rabbit was, mistakenly, passed over for the nanny to hold in her arms with the baby. She paused a moment longer in front of Miss Quigley.

"Yes," she said. "This has to be the nanny. See how professional she looks!

"And these," she said, as she inspected Sir Magnus with his white mustache and nodded her approval of Tulip's prim little mouth, "must be the grandparents."

When she came to Appleby, lying so peacefully in her bed, she smiled.

"It's a tableau," she said. "Here is the sick daughter near to death, and all the family is gathered round to pray for her recovery."

Albert and Lorna watched from the doorway. They were well aware that Daisy was not really speaking to them, just voicing her thoughts out loud, the way people who live alone are apt to do.

"She's nice," said Lorna quietly, hearing the affection in Daisy's voice.

"I know," said Albert. "And she's clever. You can see it in her eyes. If anybody can help us, she can."

Daisy, her inspection complete, looked toward the doorway.

"I'll take them," she said. "All of them."

This instant commitment startled Albert and Lorna. They had expected a tour of the house to be followed by a frank discussion of what Daisy could hope to achieve in helping to clear it. They had not expected her to be so definite about anything, least of all the dolls.

"I don't know whether you can," said Lorna, feeling very much at sea. "We don't want to sell them. And we don't want anybody else to sell them. Albert did explain to you, didn't he?"

"He explained," said Daisy.

"We need someone with plenty of space to . . . to take care of them," said Lorna. "They are very, very special. But they aren't ever to be for sale. It's a hard condition to meet."

Daisy, tired of standing, sat down on the foot of Appleby's bed. Lorna, following suit, sat in the chair that Soobie had left vacant.

"I know all of that," said Daisy. Her hand strayed to Appleby's and she took it in hers. "If you will permit me, I shall give them a home. I shall do as their maker requested. I will love them."

She looked round the room at all the dolls, *her* dolls, and gave them all the warmest of smiles, and still she held on to Appleby's hand. To love Kate's People would be so easy and so joyful.

Lorna and Albert watched her, sitting there with her outdoor coat buttoned up to the chin, a dark green coat with a little velvet collar and a golden lizard brooch in the lapel. She had not even removed the felt hat that was held on with a large hatpin. Yet there was no incongruity, no lack of dignity. Daisy Maughan could never be other than dignified. Her height, her years, and her lack of beauty were irrelevant.

"We don't need to look at anything else just now," she said. "This changes everything. I think we'd better go downstairs and talk business."

Daisy talking business was another revelation. She knew exactly what she was talking about. She knew how to dispose of everything and how to get the best prices for the goods entrusted to her. Best of all, she knew precisely what she wanted to do with the dolls.

"It will take time," she said, "but I shall work a transformation."

Lorna looked startled. It was an odd word to use!

"Don't you worry," said Daisy. "Leave it all to me."

Lorna began to feel nervous. Daisy was moving too fast. Lorna wanted to slow things down, to have time to think it out. She gripped the blue clipboard.

"Strictly speaking," she said, "everything in this house is my mother's. I think I would have to ask her first."

Daisy gave her a shrewd look.

"I won't rob you, my dear," she said. "You'll get a fair price for anything I decide to keep, and a proper price, minus commission, for whatever I sell. It will all be written down."

Lorna blushed. She was too young yet to know that one can entertain angels unawares. But she was learning.

"I'm sorry," she said. "I don't mean to imply that I doubt you. It's just that I feel responsible. I want to do things properly. You do see that, don't you?"

Albert, whose heart would always rule his head, said simply, "We'll let Daisy see to everything. She knows what she's about."

By the time the taxi took their visitor away, all the necessary decisions had been made.

❧28❧

Settling Up

In the months that followed, Albert popped in to see Daisy a few times, and sat with her sociably over a cup of tea in the little kitchen behind the showroom.

"All of the china's gone," said Daisy on his first visit, "and the clocks. I can prepare an account for them and make payment today. It won't take me a minute."

"No," said Albert. "There's no need. We'll wait till the whole house is cleared completely and then you can pay over whatever is due. But, remember, Jennifer wants nothing for the dolls, just to know that they'll have a good home. And that's what Lorna wants too. They hardly ever agree on anything, but they're in total agreement about that."

Daisy nodded and said, "Well, when it is finished, I'll let them be the judge of whether the dolls have a good home or not. For now, ask me no questions, I'll tell you no lies."

"You wouldn't anyway," said Albert.

"No," said Daisy with a laugh. "I wouldn't. People say daft things, don't they?"

But from then on, Albert waited to be told whatever Daisy chose to tell him.

"I think you'd better not sell the curtains yet," she

said. "Jennifer can have them taken down when she is ready to move in. I think it's safer to leave the place looking lived in. No curtains is a real giveaway."

Finally, at the beginning of May, Daisy said, "I think it's about time your wife and your mother-in-law paid me a visit. After next Tuesday, the house in Brocklehurst Grove will be completely empty, right to the floorboards. If all goes according to plan, I can settle up and hand back the keys."

"Magnificent," said Albert. "I don't know what we would have done without you."

He did not ask about the dolls. He knew that Daisy would tell all when she was good and ready!

And so it was that one fine Wednesday afternoon in May, Albert and Lorna drove down to North Shore Road. Leaving the car in a side street, they walked down a short steep slope, turned right, and there, a few yards along the road, was Daisy's shop. The sign on the shop door said CLOSED, but that was for customers, not for friends.

Lorna had never visited the shop, though she had heard all about it.

"Come in," said Daisy, opening the rattly shop door. "Come in and welcome."

She led them to the octagonal table which, for the occasion, had been cleared of filing boxes and was now covered with a white lace-bordered cloth. In the center, there was a silver teapot on a matching stand. A tiered cake dish was filled with scones and cream cakes, and either side of it was a large plate full of triangular sandwiches.

"There," said Daisy. "Before we talk business, let's have tea."

The table was set for four.

"Where's your mother?" said Daisy, looking at Lorna. "I was looking forward to meeting her."

"I did pass on your invitation," said Albert hastily, "but Jennifer . . ."

"Jennifer is Jennifer," Lorna interrupted. "Sometimes she shuts things out. All she wants to know about the whole business is that Aunt Kate's dying wish has been respected. Apart from that, she doesn't want to see or hear of the dolls, or anything else that was left behind, ever again. She wants to go to Number 5 Brocklehurst Grove and find it empty."

"Does she believe in ghosts?" said Daisy as she poured tea into each cup. "Is she superstitious? It's surprising how many people are."

"I don't think it's as simple as that," said Lorna. She was about to try to explain, but Daisy stopped her. She smiled, held out a plate to Lorna and said, "Come on then. Eat these sandwiches. That's what they were made for!"

After tea, Lorna and Albert cleared the table, then carefully folded the white cloth, while Daisy got out the invoices for all the items she had sold, or purchased for her own use, from the house in Brocklehurst Grove. It was a very orderly file, containing all of Lorna's original lists, ticked and cross-referenced so that everything could be easily traced.

"Following your instructions, I haven't paid you for the dolls," said Daisy when they had all sat down again at the octagonal table, "but I have entered a payment for the clothes they were wearing. If, after seeing my efforts, you should wish to dispose of the dolls in some other way, we won't exactly be back to square one, but I will have to make different arrangements."

Albert looked at one of the lists.

"The carpets fetched a good price," he said. "That's a surprise."

"They were very good quality," said Daisy. "I almost bought them myself, but recarpeting would have been wasteful."

Neither Lorna nor Albert thought to ask what she meant.

"You've bought rather a lot of the furniture yourself," said Lorna, looking doubtfully at another sheet, "and you've given us a very good price. Are you sure it's worth as much as that?"

Lorna's insistence on a fair deal worked both ways. She was rigorous about not being cheated, but equally determined not to cheat.

"Yes," said Daisy firmly. "I paid exactly what it would be expected to fetch if I sold it in the shop, minus commission as shown. So I'm happy if you are."

Lorna looked at the final total, the amount she would be taking home for her mother. It was much larger than either she or Albert had expected.

"It's a lot," said Lorna. "You've done very well."

"I've not been the loser," said Daisy. "But I can't make the check out yet—not until I know you approve of my provision for the dolls."

Albert gave her a quizzical look.

Daisy smiled.

"I'm a hard-headed businesswoman," she said. "If I don't get to keep the dolls, I won't be paying for their clothing, now, will I?"

Albert wasn't sure whether she was joking or not.

Lorna looked at her shrewdly and said, "In that case, Daisy, our next step must be to see the dolls again. Where have you taken them?"

She looked round the shop. Apart from the little kitchen which had been built onto the back, there appeared to be no other room in the shop, not even a stockroom. The floor space extended the full width and depth of the building.

Daisy stood up and went to the coat stand in the corner. She put on a short outdoor jacket and buttoned it up as if ready for an outing. She grasped her stick and began to walk toward the doorway.

"Have we far to go?" said Albert. "The car's just up the lane. I thought it best not to park in front of the shop in case it caused an obstruction."

Daisy laughed.

"We're going next door," she said. "No further than that. But if I leave the shop, I like to look as if I'm going out, be it ever so short a trip."

They went out and Daisy carefully locked up, then led them along the street past the window where Lily Waggons was seated at her sewing machine. There, between the window of the antique shop and the brown-painted window of a painters' merchant's, was an ordinary house door with an aged doorstep trodden hollow in the middle. Painted in gilt figures on the fanlight was the number thirty-nine. Daisy selected the right key on her key ring and opened the door.

"This time," she said, "it's me to go first. It might not be good manners, and it's not good sense—you'll have to be patient as you follow me up the stairs—but I've a surprise for you and I want to enjoy it!"

❦ 29 ❦

The Dolls' House

They stood at the foot of a steep staircase. About twenty stairs led up to the floor above the shop. A dark-colored, narrow carpet was held in place by thick wooden stair rods. The wood to either side of it was painted deep cream.

"You see what I mean," said Daisy. "It's no easy climb."

She led the way nonetheless, holding onto the highly polished handrail that was bolted to the side wall. Lorna and Albert followed. Daisy trod on each stair with both feet like a young child. It was, as she had warned them, painfully slow.

When they reached the top, they found themselves on a square landing from which another equally long and steep staircase led to a floor above. Daisy paused for breath, then walked into the hallway to the right of the landing. She looked nervous.

"This way," she said, in tones that sounded almost hushed. "Look at everything as we go, but say nothing. Save your words till we go down again."

The first room they went into was amazing. A living room, quite large, with two long windows facing over the river. And, apart from the carpet, every item in the room had come from the lounge at Number 5 Brocklehurst Grove. Seated at the round table in the corner were two figures that looked as if they were sharing a magazine, elbows on the table, heads bent to look at the page. Pilbeam and Appleby were posed as in life, like real teenagers spending an afternoon at home. Daisy had dressed them in some of the teenage clothes that had come from the wardrobes in Brocklehurst Grove. It was wonderful how good a fit they were! Nearly all of the clothes there had proved useful, one way or another. Only the clothes that had once belonged to Sir Magnus had eventually found a place in the shop window's theatrical display. The naval uniform had been snapped up almost immediately.

The suite arranged around the fireplace was the one where the older Mennyms used to sit when it occupied the same spot in Brocklehurst Grove. On the hearth rug in front of the fire knelt a doll with fair curls tied in bunches, apparently playing with a smaller doll. But Wimpey was in no condition now to pull the string that would make Polly talk.

The next room they went into was the kitchen. It was a very old-fashioned kitchen with a deep chipped sink in one corner. There was a single brass tap, cold water only, and a draining board of grooved wood, which had been scrubbed till it was almost white. There was an old iron range: a fireplace with a side oven and, beneath it, a water boiler. The range was well blackened and the tap to the boiler was of shiny brass. On the hob in front of the fire stood a big old kettle, the sort that a pot could fairly call black. No fire, of course. Daisy still lit one occasionally, and would certainly be tempted to do so again. But, for now, no fire. In this room too all of the furniture had been brought from Brocklehurst Grove. Beside the kitchen table, at the ironing board, stood the doll that had once been Vinetta, her right hand resting heavily on the iron as she appeared to press a shirt. On a kitchen chair sat Joshua, a brush in one hand, a shoe perched on the other, and on a stool beside him was a tin of Cherry Blossom Boot Polish.

There were two more rooms on this floor, a small bedroom next to the kitchen (for the nanny), and a larger room next to the living room, which Daisy had decided should be the nursery, complete with Googles's own cot and playpen. In there, Miss Quigley was seated in a large armchair holding the baby over her shoulder and appearing to be in the act of patting its back. The playpen was folded up against the wall and in a pile beside it were various toys, including the floppy-eared rabbit that had once belonged to Poopie.

"Now for the next floor," said Daisy, and they were the first words spoken since they entered the flat. She was eyeing both of them anxiously, but, obedient to her wish, they remained silent.

They went back to the landing and climbed the next flight of stairs. On this landing too there were four rooms. No bathroom, of course. Just four plain rooms, two large, one medium and one very small. In the large front bedroom, arranged with wonderful insight, Sir Magnus lay in his bed propped up by pillows and apparently reading a book. His purple feet were both well hidden under the counterpane. Apart from that, he might well have been at home. In the armchair beside him, holding a pair of knitting needles, as if in the middle of making a little pink garment, was Tulip. The knitting itself was, of course, Daisy's own work. She was not a skilled knitter and goodness knows how Tulip would have felt if she had been able to look down at it!

The large back bedroom was filled with all of the things from the room that Vinetta and Joshua had shared for half a century or more. In the medium-sized bedroom next to it were three beds and an assortment of girls' things gathered from Pilbeam's, Appleby's and Wimpey's old rooms. Not everything had been kept. There wasn't space. Number 39 North Shore Road was a large flat with high-ceilinged old-fashioned rooms, but it was nowhere near the size of the house in Brocklehurst Grove.

In the small bedroom next to Granpa's room, Poopie, dressed in sweatshirt and jeans, was on the floor playing with Action Men. Daisy thought she had given the toys of an unknown child, now far away, to a doll the right shape and size. He reminded her of her brother. The whole place, filled with figures, brought back memories of happy days gone by. The only thing that did not quite fit its setting was Miss Quigley. The Maughans had never employed anyone to look after *their* children.

"It's just like old times. Though we'd never have had a nanny," said Daisy with a laugh, when she returned with Albert and Lorna to the shop below. "My mother would have had a fit at the very thought. Strangers in the house! Knowing your business! Talking about you to folk outside! I remember when I was about eight years old, I was outside the shop and a neighbor stopped and spoke to me. Do you know what my mam did? She came to the window, rapped hard at me and shooed the poor woman away. She was a character, my mam!''

Albert knew that Daisy was talking nervously. She had shown them her work, her wonderful work, and she was terrified that they wouldn't approve. She had had helpers, naturally, in moving the furniture about, but she had given hours and hours of thought to what should go where. She had arranged and rearranged the dolls in various positions, in various rooms. And every time she moved a doll she became more and more attached to it. If these young people turned round and said it wasn't what they had in mind, Daisy would be heartbroken.

Albert looked at her kindly and knew what she was thinking.

"It's tremendous,'' he said, "almost miraculous. You've brought that flat up there to life. It's a museum, a living museum.''

"Not quite that,'' said Daisy modestly, and she still looked anxiously at Lorna.

"What do *you* think?'' she said.

Lorna gave Daisy a hug before answering.

"If I had searched the length and breadth of England, I could not have found a more beautiful home, or a better carer, for Aunt Kate's People. Thank you.''

Daisy gave a sigh of relief and said, "I'll go and get my checkbook.''

"What will you do with them?'' said Lorna when Daisy returned.

"Do with them?'' said Daisy, looking up from the paperwork.

"Will you show them? That flat up there could be a show house, a theme museum. You could charge people to come and look round. It would be one way of getting some return on the money you've invested."

Daisy's eyes twinkled.

"I'm a fairly wealthy woman, by my standards," she said. "I'm sixty-eight years old and still working. I don't need to look for an extra source of income."

"So what will you do?" said Albert, genuinely interested and suspecting that the answer might be surprising.

"I'll spend a lot of time there, especially in the summer evenings," said Daisy. "What was once my first home will be my second home now. I'll bring the dolls into the living room to watch the television with me. I'll sit them round the table and pretend we're having a meal together. I'm even planning to install a chairlift on those stairs to make my visiting easier. It will be my dolls' house. I'll be set for my second childhood."

Lorna, taking her literally, looked worried.

"No," said Daisy, seeing the expression on Lorna's face. "I'm not in my dotage or anywhere near it! It'll be my game. Old men play golf, or sit in the park over huge games of draughts or chess. Even the games young people play are only just this side of daft, if you think about it. Playing with dolls is no worse than kicking a ball about."

"Still," said Albert, "it seems a shame if no one ever sees what you've done."

"Kate Penshaw was the real artist," said Daisy. "I am just the window dresser. But I didn't say no one would ever see the dolls in their new home. I will show them to friends and old customers and children. But I couldn't turn it into a business any more than I could sell the wooden betty dolls out of my shop window.''

After that, the business side was soon completed.

"We'll see ourselves out," said Albert. "You just sit and rest."

As they were leaving, a couple with a young boy started to come in.

"The shop's closed," said Lorna. "We're not customers."

"Neither are we," said the man with a smile that reminded her of Daisy. "We're family. We've come to see Aunt Daisy."

The Ponds returned with the good news to Elmtree Road, taking with them the check which Jennifer had perversely insisted should be made out to Lorna. When they got there, they found the reason why.

"I'll pay this into the bank tomorrow," said Lorna, "and have it transferred to your account as soon as it clears."

"No," said Jennifer, "you won't do that. You must keep it. You and Albert have done all the work, and I did say that I had no wish to benefit from the things that family left behind."

"Mother!" said Lorna. "That's a large sum of money. We couldn't possibly keep it."

"You could, you can and you will," said Jennifer. "If I can't give money to my own daughter, who can I give it to? And don't say you and Albert don't need it. University salaries don't leave much over after you've paid the bills, especially now you have a baby to keep.''

"What about the others?" said Lorna, trying as always to be fair.

"That's up to you," said Jennifer. "Entirely up to you."

❧ 30 ❧

Billy

The street that ran alongside the marketplace in Castledean was full of small, practical shops, shabby but serviceable. Among them were two or three cafés, ranging from a newly built Kentucky Fried Chicken restaurant at the top end of the street to a very run-down sandwich bar at the bottom. When the Maughans, Jamie and Molly and their son Billy, came in from the country, they always went to the curtained little café where there were waitresses serving at the tables and each table had a proper tablecloth with a small bunch of flowers in a silver vase in the center.

Billy was sitting with his mam and dad at a table near the window. His shoulder kept brushing against a rubber plant that looked as if it might like to join in the conversation. It certainly looked more talkative than Billy.

"You're very quiet today, Billy," said his mother as she poured another cup of tea for each of them. "Is something upsetting you?"

Billy looked awkward. At thirteen, he was beginning to feel too old to think that a day out in town with his mother and father was much of a treat. It had been at one time. It had been a treat for years and years. But now he felt as if he was getting too old to be taken out shopping.

"Would you like anything else?" said the waitress, smiling down at Billy.

"A knickerbocker glory?" said his mother, looking at her son hopefully.

"I suppose so," said Billy. Then, unable to break the good habits of a lifetime, he added, "Yes, please."

He would rather have refused the treat, but it is very hard to say no to a knickerbocker glory.

"Well, cheer up then," said his mother. She smiled at the waitress, a plump middle-aged woman who knew what kids were like.

"There's no pleasing them sometimes," she said, and went off to fetch the order.

Jamie and Molly drank more tea while Billy made his way down the glass of ice cream, trying his hardest to look as if he were not particularly enjoying it.

"Can we go home now?" he said as soon as he had finished. "If we're back quick I can call on Joe and see if he wants to go for a ride."

Jamie Maughan looked grim. He did not like Joe Dorward. He had never liked Joe Dorward. The lad was two years older than Billy and though not quite a criminal, certainly what Jamie would call "a slippery customer." And Jamie did not know the half of it! Joe had led Billy into a variety of sticky situations that included spending the hours meant for sleep prowling around the countryside playing at detectives. And on one memorable night, three years ago, Joe and Billy had seen something they would never forget. They had gone spying around a country house. There they had seen a life-sized blue rag doll which they kidnapped to burn on the bonfire for Guy Fawkes. Then they had discovered that the doll could walk and talk and run and jump and . . . wave good-bye! No one knew about it, of course. It was a secret never to be told.

"I wish you'd stop away from that lad," said Jamie. "He's bad news. One day he'll get himself into real trouble—and you'n all, if you let him."

Molly looked at the two of them. Billy was small for his age but wiry. His ginger hair had been sleeked down that morning but was looking tousled as ever by now. Jamie had the same coloring as his son but his hair was darker ginger, thicker and cut close to the scalp. He was short and stocky. He was usually full of fun, enjoying a joke, even a feeble one, but his rules of behavior were never a joking matter. He could be very strict when he felt that the occasion called for it.

"We'll not have any arguments about Joe Dorward," said Molly firmly. "We've been over it all again and again. And we aren't going straight home anyway, Billy. You know we aren't. We're going to see Aunt Daisy, like we usually do. You like Aunt Daisy, don't you? She's always very kind to you, and very pleased to see you."

It was impossible to deny that. Billy shrugged his shoulders. He did like Aunt Daisy and he knew she was always nice to him. But he was thirteen and he wanted to grow up and they just wouldn't let him. How could he grow up without being nasty to people? It was a hard problem. Sometimes he thought it was one he'd never solve. Joe Dorward was always arguing with *his* mam and dad. Sometimes he even walked out on them and slammed the door. Then he'd go back and they'd all be friends again, just as if nothing had happened.

Billy wasn't made that way. He was as brave as the next lad, but he couldn't bring himself to be out and out cheeky. He was too worried about upsetting his mam. So he said no more and walked with his parents down from the marketplace into the long street that led under the railway viaduct to the road that ran by the river. They arrived at the door of Aunt Daisy's shop just as Albert and Lorna were leaving.

"The shop's closed," said Lorna. "We're not customers."

"Neither are we," said Jamie with a smile. "We're family. We've come to see Aunt Daisy."

Billy passed by Albert, brushing his sleeve. He looked up at him and saw a face he felt was familiar. But three years is a long time, and he had seen Albert briefly only twice. Lorna smiled at Molly. Then she and Albert went on their way.

"Jamie!" said Daisy, rising slowly from her seat as she saw her cousin's son and his family enter. She grasped her stick and walked to meet them. "With all the business I've been up to, I clean forgot it was today you were coming."

"Well, we'll go out and come back, if you like," joked Jamie. "Give you time to collect your scattered wits."

"Cheeky!" said Daisy. "Come on through to the back and sit yourselves down. I've plenty of leftovers from the tea we've just had. And I'll soon make you a nice cuppa."

"It's all right, Aunt Daisy," said Molly, "we've just eaten."

"Nonsense," said Daisy, filling the kettle and plugging it into the point on the wall, "you've got to have a cup of tea now you're here."

The back kitchen had been built on some years ago. It was small but it had a cooker, a sink, a fridge, a set of sturdy kitchen chairs and a big square table. It was less formal than entertaining at the octagonal table in the shop with the lace-edged cloth and the silver tea service. But Jamie was family.

The Maughans drank tea and even managed to eat some of the cakes and sandwiches, feeling that Daisy would be disappointed if they didn't.

"Now," said Daisy, after they had declared that they could eat and drink no more, "I have a surprise for you. A big surprise."

She was clearly excited, the expression on her face as young as Billy's.

They all looked at her expectantly.

Daisy got up slowly and made her way toward the coat stand.

"Well, where are we going?" said Molly as she saw her take down her outdoor coat.

"Just upstairs," said Daisy, "to the flat. But you know me by now. If I go out I like to have my coat on."

"Been buying something big?" said Jamie, knowing that the flat had long been used as a storeroom.

"Bigger than you can possibly imagine," said Daisy with a laugh.

❧ 31 ❧

Just a Memory

"**S**o where is it?" said Jamie.

All four were standing at the top of the stairs in the flat above Daisy's shop. The doors around them were closed.

"What is it?" asked Billy, beginning to feel curious in spite of himself. Inside every thirteen-year-old there's a ten-year-old fighting to regain lost ground.

Daisy smiled up at him. Small he might be, but he was still a bit taller than Aunt Daisy.

"It's a dolls' house," said Daisy.

"A dolls' house!" said Billy in tones of disgust. "Them's just for little girls. I thought you had something really interesting!"

"Don't be so bad-mannered, Billy," said his mother. "A dolls' house can be very valuable if it's old and special. It can be a collector's piece. And your Aunt Daisy would know all about that if anybody would."

"Well, where is it?" said Jamie.

"Here," said Daisy, indicating all of the doors with a wave of one plump arm.

"What do you mean?" said Jamie.

"I'll show you."

She opened the door that led to the kitchen.

Vinetta was still standing there, frozen in the act of ironing.

As Billy looked at her, he felt a shiver. He had never seen her before, or anyone precisely like her. But she was somehow familiar, recognizable as a special sort of rag doll, generic with at least two that he *had* seen before. The recognition was imprecise and fleeting, but Billy stood still, staring at her.

Daisy looked at him, amused.

"Dumbstruck?" she said. "Thought you might be."

She went closer to Vinetta.

"This is Mrs. Mennym," she said. "I call my family Mennym after the people who have looked after them for the past fifty years or so. This one's first name is Agatha. I haven't named all of the others yet. I want to get names with the right flavor."

They went to the living room. Jamie and Molly exclaimed on the furnishings and the dolls at the table and on the floor.

"Last time I saw this place it was a total shambles, all boxes and crates and what-have-you," said Jamie. "There's some work gone into this, not to mention money."

"Did it all meself," said Daisy, and then laughed at Billy, whose face was a picture.

"We-ell," she added, "I did have some help. It's a few years since I packed in the weight lifting!"

Billy didn't know quite what to say. So he said nothing.

Daisy lifted the girl doll from the hearth rug and sat

it on a chair. Then she held up the American doll and pulled its string.

"My-name-is-Polly," said the doll. "What-is-your-name?"

Daisy pulled the string again.

"Would-you-like-a-chocolate-milk?" asked the doll.

"This is just a shop doll," said Daisy. "No more than ten years old, if that. I'll tell you the whole story of where they all came from and how they're all here, when we go downstairs again."

Billy looked across at the girl doll in the chair, golden hair tied in bunches, and suddenly he knew! He had seen Wimpey skipping along the path in front of Comus House. That was three years ago, but it was a strongly etched memory, part of that series of events that he would never forget. If this was not the same doll, it was certainly the work of the same factory that turned them out. Daisy saw him looking.

"I've called that one Miranda," she said, "but I haven't fixed on any names for her sisters yet. It all takes time."

"Where did you buy them?" said Billy. "Did you get them from up our way? In Allenbridge mebbe?"

"No," said Daisy with a long, slow "no" that implied that such a thought was ridiculous. "We'll see the rest of them first. Then we'll go back to the shop for a natter and another cup of tea."

When the story was told, Billy was none the wiser. He did not mention his memory of any of them. He did not want them asking questions. Goodness knows where questions might lead! But he kept on thinking and thinking as he trailed behind his parents on the road up to the car park.

Billy was sitting in the front seat next to his dad, and was still trying hard to think of some way of getting back to Aunt Daisy's on his own. They were a few miles out of Castledean, nearly within sight of Tidy Hill, when Molly gave him the idea he had been looking for.

"You've been very quiet all day, Billy," she said, talking from the backseat over her husband's shoulder. "If there's something wrong, say. You know *I* always listen."

Billy knew only too well what the emphasis meant. His dad was no listener!

"I wish you'd let me be like other lads," said Billy. "There's kids in my class go all over the place by themselves. Jimmy Reed's no bigger than me—and he's two months younger—but his ma lets him go on his own to see his gran in Rimstead every other Sunday. Me, I can never go anywhere on me own!"

"Don't say 'ma,' " said Molly. "It sounds common."

"You're as bad as *he* is," said Billy. "You're not listening to me at all."

"Call me what you like, so long as you call me," said Jamie, trying to make a joke of it.

"Shut up, Jamie," said Molly. "I'm sorry, Billy. I know what you're trying to say. But I'm not sure what you want me to do about it."

"Just trust me a bit more," said Billy eagerly. "Let me come into Castledean by meself. I'll not get lost, y'know. You're worse for gettin' lost than I am."

"Where would you go?" said Molly.

"I could go to Aunt Daisy's and see the dolls again," he said. "That would do for a start."

"You said that dolls were just for girls," Jamie reminded him.

"Not them dolls," said Billy. "They're too big. They're like figures in a waxworks museum."

"They're made of cloth, not wax," said Jamie.

"I know *that,*" said Billy, "but you know what I mean. Mam does."

He looked at his mother for support.

"I know," said Molly, "and I don't see why you shouldn't go and see them again—on your own. Next Saturday maybe."

"How would he get there?" said Jamie. "By bus? It's not as easy as coming down in the car. I won't have time to fetch him back, either."

"I don't want you to fetch me, Dad, and I don't want you to take me," said Billy loudly. "I want to go there and back, by meself, on the bus, like any other person would."

"So you're a person now?" said Jamie. "A proper-sized person, ready to take on the world?"

That was too much for Molly.

"Yes, he's a person. Hadn't you realized?" she said, irritation showing in her voice. "You can go on Saturday, Billy. I'll give you the fare, and I'll leave you to find out the bus times yourself. I would like to know what bus you'll be getting back, that's all."

"He'll be off gallivantin' with that Joe Dorward, I'd like to bet," growled Jamie.

"No, he'll not," said Molly. "I trust him, if you don't. By yourself means by yourself, doesn't it, Billy?"

"It needn't," said Billy, anxious not to commit himself for future outings, "not always. But this time it will. I'll not even tell Joe where I'm going."

32

The Empty House

On Friday after tea, Albert and Lorna left Matthew with his grandmother once more and went to pay a visit to Number 5 Brocklehurst Grove. Some day soon, Jennifer would have to be persuaded to inspect and approve the empty house. No one in the family was sure whether she would ever agree to live there, no matter what plans had been made.

"I'd like to go and look at it, now that it's empty," said Lorna. "I'd like to try and see it through my mother's eyes. She can be very unreasonable at times."

"Can't we all?" said Albert, the most reasonable of men.

"Well," said Lorna, "in this case it is Mother's unreasonableness that is our concern. And in case you've a mind to go all scholarly and pedantic on me, it is her unreasonableness with regard to moving house. She knows it will be for the best, but to my mind she is still dragging her feet."

So Albert and Lorna took on the responsibility of looking at Number 5, checking that everything was in order.

They let themselves in by the front door and saw at once that the job had been done very thoroughly. The wood boards of the floor were spotlessly clean. A faded patch on the wall showed where the mirror had hung. Outlines of departed pictures and furniture were all they saw as they inspected each room in the house. Even the picture hooks had been carefully removed from the walls. There were still bulbs in the ceiling lights, but every lampshade had gone.

Lorna and Albert were aware of their footsteps ringing loudly on the bare floorboards. It was not an eerie sound, rather the reverse, healthy, robust and assertive. The Mennyms, they felt, were well and truly ousted, like ghosts that have been exorcised.

"She should be satisfied," said Lorna as they walked along the top landing. "This is as empty a house as anyone could hope to find. It can be redecorated from top to bottom before they move in."

But then they came to the staircase at the end of the landing, the narrow, half-hidden staircase that led to the attic.

"Oh!" said Lorna abruptly. "We never looked up there. It could need clearing."

"Daisy might have done it," said Albert.

"I doubt it," said Lorna. "She would only take the things that were on the checklists we gave her. If she found anything else she would have said. *You* must know that. You know her better than I do."

"We'd better go up there and have a look," said Albert. "With a bit of luck, we'll find only water tanks and pipework."

They climbed the narrow staircase and stood outside the attic door. Its wedge shape, one side longer than the other, made it look more like the door to a cupboard.

"We might not be able to see much," said Albert as he turned the door handle.

But as the door opened, they saw pale shafts of evening sunlight slanting down from two dusty skylights in the roof. They found themselves looking at a great space spreading beneath the rafters to the wall at the gable end of the house. The air was musty. Cobwebs like fragile stalactites hung down from the underside of the roof. The area beyond the skylights was deep in gloom. In a socket attached to the central rafter was a light bulb, unlit of course.

Albert and Lorna looked helplessly at the mess. The floor space was covered with all sorts of objects that would need closer inspection. And the attic was growing darker by the minute.

"We'll have to switch on the light," said Lorna. "Can you see the switch anywhere?"

Albert found it just outside the door.

"Good job we didn't have the power turned off," he said.

The bulb was not very strong, but it gave enough light for them to see things a bit more clearly. In front of them, slightly to their left, they saw the back of a big old-fashioned wooden rocking chair. Over it was draped a dark-gray knitted blanket. Just visible beside it was a velvet footstool with little, curved legs. Albert and Lorna walked into the room.

And then they saw the big rag doll, lying in the rocking chair.

Lorna stepped back, startled. The hand that hung over edge of the chair arm was made of blue cloth. The foot on the footstool was wearing ordinary trainers, such as any young man might wear. But the head, oddly tilted and partly sunk on its chest, was all blue, except for a pair of silver button eyes that she could fancy were looking at her. The doll was well padded and wearing a blue tracksuit trimmed with white. Dust had settled on it, but not as thickly as on the other objects in the room.

Lorna, with all her knowledge of the dolls that had been found in the room below, quickly recovered.

"If my mother saw that," she said, "she would never move in here at all."

"I can't say I'd blame her," said Albert. "It is unnerving. Why was this one not with the others? Why did they care for the rest and leave this one all on its own?"

Lorna went up to the chair and looked at the doll more closely.

"It *has* been cared for," she said. "That tracksuit is quite new. The doll itself is clean and neat under that layer of dust. It can't have been here all that long. It's hard to fathom."

"Perhaps they put this one out of the way because of its blue face," said Albert. "It doesn't match the others at all, does it?"

"Except that it's another rag doll," said Lorna, "and presumably it too was made by Aunt Kate."

She raised the doll's head and straightened its torso into a more lifelike position. Then, ever a champion of the underdog, she began to feel sorry for this doll that had not been considered good enough to place with the others. With her hands she gently brushed the dust from its blue face. She began to think of a name for it, wondering what one could call a doll that was different.

"We'll have to see Daisy about it," she said. "Daisy will understand. She'll find a place for this one, perhaps a better place than all the rest."

Albert smiled. Sometimes, he thought, people have to grow down to grow up!

They went on to lift the lid of a wicker chest where they found rolls of material in all sorts of shades and patterns. They looked at a dolls' house that must have been nearly a hundred years old. Pilbeam's mirror on its stand was still there and the packing case full of jumble. Lorna picked up a copy of *Bleak House* from a small pile of books.

"Fancy putting these up here," she said, eyeing it with a librarian's interest. "No book deserves to be banished like that."

"I think we should leave everything for now," said Albert. "I'll give Daisy a ring and explain. But I won't have time to take the keys down to North Shore Road till next weekend. Unless you'd like to go?"

"No, Albert," said Lorna, "she's your friend really. She'll be pleased to see you again. There's no hurry anyway. I'll tell my mother that the attic has still to be cleared out. If I know her, she'll be glad of the excuse to put off coming here again."

"That's not fair," said Albert.

"It's perfectly fair," said Lorna. "She just doesn't want to make up her mind."

"Or have it made up for her," said Albert softly.

❦ 33 ❧

Where's the Blue One?

Billy walked across Castledean High Street and immediately crossed back again. He was going to see Aunt Daisy, all on his own, for the very first time. He decided to take her a present. So he went to the Chocolate Cabin and bought her a box of fudge with a picture of a castle on the lid. It was not much of a present, but it was all he could afford. His mam had always told him that what counted was the thought.

After that, he hurried as fast as he could down to the shop by the river. When he arrived he found that Aunt Daisy had customers, at least three of them looking at different items in the shop.

"Your mam said you were coming," said Daisy as he came through the door. "I'm a bit busy now, but I'll give you the key and you can pop upstairs to the flat. I'm not kidding myself it's me you came to see! I'll be up in an hour or so when I close for lunch."

She had the key ready in the pocket of her tweed skirt.

"You can rearrange them if you like," she said, not using the word "dolls" and cleverly saying "rearrange" instead of "play with." Not for the world would she embarrass Billy in front of strangers. Though the strangers were not taking much notice anyway. They were too busy inspecting their prospective purchases, inside, outside, and upside down.

"I know you'll be careful with them," she added as she handed Billy the key.

He took it from her, smiled shyly, and thrust his gift into her hand as he made for the door.

"That's for you," he said.

"From your mam?" said Daisy.

"No," said Billy. "I got it for you meself. It's the thought that counts."

"Thank you, love," said Daisy, looking down at the box. "The thought is appreciated, and I can enjoy the fudge as well!"

Daisy had already been playing with the dolls, perhaps one should say "rearranging" them. In the living room, Joshua was sitting in an armchair, with Vinetta on an identical chair beside him. Wimpey was seated cross-legged on the floor in front of them. The older girls were sitting on smaller chairs. And they were all facing the television set in the corner.

Billy went across and switched it on.

"You might as well be watching something," he said, "instead of just sitting there!"

It was an expression he had learned from Joe Dorward's mum, one he had always fancied using.

He picked up the shop doll from the settee, pulled the string and heard the voice, then placed it on the little girl's knee. He couldn't help looking wistfully at the one face he felt sure he knew. It was impossible. These dolls belonged to Castledean. They had never been anywhere near Allenbridge. They had certainly never been inside the place they called Comus House. It had to be a different doll. It just *had* to be . . . and yet?

Next he went to the nursery where Nanny was sitting nursing the baby and feeding her "milk" from an empty bottle. Against the nursery wall, an old playpen made of polished wood was still folded up. Billy put it in the center of the floor, had a performance a bit like his dad trying to set up a deck chair on the beach, and eventually turned it into a functional object.

"Here," he said to the baby, lifting her out of her nanny's arms. "I bet you'd like to play in there." He sat the baby up in one corner of the playpen so that her back was well supported. Then he looked around the room, found a large ball that had a carousel inside it and played a tune as it moved. He passed it over the frame into the baby's arms. Next he found the rabbit that had once belonged to Poopie. That too was put into the playpen before Billy passed on to look at the other rooms and other dolls.

He came to the room that had been allocated to the little boy doll. Here he spent the rest of his time as he waited for Aunt Daisy. Only he wasn't waiting. He was playing for all his worth and had forgotten his aunt completely.

When he went in he found the doll sitting on the floor with its back against the bed. It was surrounded by Action Man equipment and in one hand it was holding an Action Man that had lost an arm and looked much the worse for wear. The arrangement was artistic. But wrong, all wrong. The pieces on the floor were parts of a training tower from which the soldiers were meant to slide down ropes and then climb up to the top again. The other Action Men, arranged so neatly as if on parade, should have been on maneuvers. Billy knew that. Of course he did! It was not so very long since he'd played with toys like that himself. And wished he still did! Being thirteen is a terrible responsibility.

"You haven't a clue," he said, looking at the doll's cloth face and blue button eyes beneath pudding-basin bangs. "Move over. I'll show you how."

Billy sat down beside the boy doll and set to work. In a box at the foot of the bed he found enough equipment to make a fantastic game. By the time he had finished, the game had spread over half the room. There were hills and valleys, tents and gun-emplacements, and the training tower was erected to its full height with ropes fixed to the top and fanning out to the earth below. On one side of the tower, two soldiers, bayonets on their backs, were climbing up some netting. Beneath the tower, another two were stretched on their stomachs and taking aim at something with the rifles tucked under their arms.

"That's more like it," said Billy. "You don't deserve such marvelous toys if you don't know how to play with them. I never had half what you've got, but I made the most of them. I didn't just sit around helpless and leave things all in bits."

At that moment, Billy heard the downstairs door open and shut. He jumped up immediately and went out on to the landing. Daisy was coming slowly up the stairs. Billy ran down to meet her.

"Are you having a good time?" she asked as she

reached the first landing. "Let's see what you've been doing."

Together they went from room to room.

"You've not spent the time watching telly, have you?" she said as they went into the living room where the lunchtime news was being broadcast.

"Course not," said Billy. "The picture's not very clear anyway. I just thought that since you'd set them up facing the telly, it would look good if there was something on for them to watch."

Daisy nodded.

"Yes," she said. "You're absolutely right. It does."

Daisy was delighted with everything Billy had done. She looked at the game he had set up for Poopie.

"Some day," she said, "you'll be a wonderful dad. You have something special inside that noddle of yours. Never, ever lose it. Do you hear?"

They returned to the living room to switch off the television set.

"The news is about finished," said Daisy. "I don't suppose they'll want to see anything else just now."

Billy took one more look at the doll that Daisy called Miranda. It was uncanny. He knew her. He knew he knew her. But where was the doll he and his friends had once kidnapped? Where was the blue one?

Downstairs in the kitchen behind the shop, Daisy gave Billy tea and scones and sandwiches. She had left the SHOP CLOSED sign facing the street.

"When does your lunch hour end?" asked Billy, worried in case more customers would come and bring his visit to an early end.

"When I want it to," said Daisy with a laugh. "It's a very flexible arrangement. I don't think there'll be a queue at the door just yet. Most of my customers tell me when they're coming."

Billy did not really intend to say what he said next. He just couldn't help himself.

"The dolls upstairs," he began tentatively, "are there any more of them?"

"Not as I know of," said Daisy, looking at him curiously.

"You're sure? Is there not a blue one?"

It was the wrong question to ask Daisy. Before another half hour had passed she had wheedled out of him the whole story of the kidnapping of a blue rag doll from a house that he and his friends had thought at the time was empty. He was emphatic that the little girl doll was the doll he had seen through binoculars, skipping in front of that house in the country, near the farm where he lived. He had begun by making Daisy promise never to tell his mam and dad. He ended saying, "You do believe me, don't you?"

"Yes," said Daisy. "I do."

"You're not just saying that, are you?"

"No," said Daisy, but yes and no are not satisfactory answers. They seldom tell the full truth. Daisy knew that and so she tried to explain.

"I believe you saw what you say you saw," she said, "but I can't explain it any more than you can. I wasn't there, which makes it even harder. And, I have to say it, I am appalled at what you did. Your mam and dad take good care of you and they love you very much.

Yet you sneaked out with them other lads and got up to all sorts of mischief. And you were only ten. You were lucky nothing really bad happened.''

"I wouldn't do it *now*," said Billy anxiously. "You've promised you won't tell."

"And I'll keep my promise," said Daisy, "but you'll have to promise me something."

"What?" said Billy, hoping it wouldn't be something too hard.

"You're not to tell any of those lads about the flat above the shop and the dolls I've got there."

"I won't, Aunt Daisy. Honest I won't. I won't even tell Joe."

"Especially Joe. He's the sort could shin up drainpipes."

A customer rattled the door.

"I'd best be goin' now," said Billy. "I don't want to be late back."

"What time's your bus?" said Daisy.

"Three o'clock," said Billy. "If I miss that one, there's not another till ten to four."

"Well, you'll be going none too soon then. But come again. Come next week if you can. I love to see you—and so do me dolls!"

Daisy was left not knowing what to think. But she made up her mind to keep a careful eye on her Mennyms, ready to detect any signs of life. She found herself wondering how she would feel if she heard noises from the flat above. Then, with an effort, she gave her full attention to the woman who had walked into the shop and was saying something about a table.

"The gate-legged table, Mrs. Woodhouse?" said Daisy. "I'm sorry. I sold it this morning. If only you'd said the other day! I'd have held onto it for you. The candlesticks are still here if you want them."

✣ 34 ✣

Soobie

And there *was* a blue one. Of course there was!

The blue rag doll sat in the rocking chair in the attic, imprisoned in stillness and silence, but living. Deep down in his being he was still alive and had never known death, just immobility.

How does a rag doll die? Sir Magnus had asked himself that question and the answer had been simple. Soobie had asked himself that question, and there had been no answer. He had sat in the rocking chair and seen the light of paradise flash through the attic. It had struck him dumb and left him paralyzed. But not dead. It was as if an anaesthetic had worked on every bit of him except his powers of perception. For months, he could not raise his head or move his limbs. Yet he could hear most acutely. He could see most clearly.

I am not to know death, he thought, as he sat in the darkness after the light that should have killed him died away. I am not to know death.

At the other side of the attic, when daylight came, he saw the door that had once been mystic and magical. Now it hung open on damaged hinges. The space behind it was a wall of bricks with old plaster oozing out of them like cream between layers of cake. Soobie felt waves of terror and emptiness and grief. But never death. Frustration and boredom and weariness. But never death.

His left arm lay across his knee. The watch on his wrist, that perfect present, told him when October became November. The house remained sealed like a tomb. And all he could hear was the noise of the wind when it howled in the chimneys, or the rain when it lashed the windowpanes.

December came. And in the second week of that month, Soobie heard someone enter the front door. It was three floors below, but the sound was unmistakable. Emotions of fear, frustration, misery and even a sort of joy invaded his spirit. For weeks there had been no sign of life in the house.

Now footsteps, heavy footsteps, could be heard making rapid progress through all the rooms. Doors opened and closed in quick succession. At last, the feet reached the bare boards of the attic staircase. Soobie was filled with terror. There had been no voices. This was a single intruder. One man, heavy-footed and purposeful.

The attic door opened. Whatever the man was doing, standing in the doorway behind him, Soobie did not know. He could not turn to see. On the floor beyond the footstool was the mirror he thought of as Pilbeam's, an old mirror hanging in a wooden frame. Through it, he could just make out the bottom of a long overcoat, and a pair of pin-striped trousers above well-polished shoes. The man stood still for a few seconds. Then he turned and went out, closing the door behind him. He would be able to put in his report that the roof appeared to be sound. But Soobie was not to know that.

Forever passed. To do nothing, nothing at all, is almost to *be* nothing. This was not watching the world as Joshua had once imagined it. The view was limited to the walls, the floor and the rafters. The only movement was that of clouds as they roamed across the sky, seen vaguely through the increasingly dusty skylight windows. Soobie's watch gave him the news that it was January. His heart was near to despair. How, oh how, does a rag doll die?

Sometimes, it seemed to him, any end would be preferable to such prolonged imprisonment. Any noise better than eternal silence. So it was wonderful to him when he heard the street door open and close once more. It was a heavy, noisy door, and Soobie could hear it quite clearly. In fact, his hearing became more acute, the less there was for him to hear.

He listened to the Gladstones going through the house. He could hear their voices and he struggled to make out what they were saying. He wondered if the rest of his family were in the same case as he, tortured by the nightmare life-in-death. He doubted it. Something told him that they were truly dead, returned to their original state of lifelessness.

Suddenly, there was an almighty yell and the sound of running feet.

"There's a room full of dead bodies," a child's voice shouted. Then Soobie knew that his family had been found. He expected to be next. They could take me to pieces, he thought. They could throw me away. And I would not be able to lift a finger. What would I feel like? Which part of me would take this life with it? For by now he felt that the life inside him must be totally indestructible. Would a piece of blue rag in a dustbin somewhere end up thinking, I am . . . and I am Soobie Mennym?

But he was left undiscovered. The family went away again without ascending to the attic.

After that there were more visits to the house. Soobie heard Albert when he called downstairs to Lorna to get her to come and see Granpa's brilliant white naval uniform. He did not recognize the voice, of course. Even acute hearing cannot be so perceptive at such a distance.

Over the next few weeks, the noises in the house became more and more frequent. In some ways, Soobie was glad to hear them. But always there was the fear that the attic might be invaded. And worse still, there was the agony of not knowing what was happening to his family on the floor below.

"Mind what you're doing, Michael," said a voice one day, a deep, man's voice, speaking loudly. (How Soobie wished they would all speak loudly. That way he might learn more.) "Them dolls have to be kept perfect. You know what madam's like. When she says perfect, she means perfect. The sooner they're properly crated up, the happier I'll be."

So, thought Soobie, with something like relief, at least someone wants to make sure that we're cared for. Only it wasn't "we," it was "they." The blue Mennym was no longer sure whether being found was the worst that could happen to him.

After that, nothing much of interest was said in the

house below. The furniture was removed and the carpets were lifted. But no one came to the attic.

"What's up these stairs, Ted?" he heard a voice say one afternoon.

"Don't know," said another voice, "but I don't care either. We've enough to do clearing this lot. We check off what's on the list. That's what we're paid for. We haven't got time to be nosing about."

For the past week, the watch had been telling Soobie that it was May. And a few days after the workmen left, Soobie received his first real visit from the world outside. The attic door opened. Then the light was switched on. And in came Albert and Lorna.

Lorna came close to him first. She sat him more comfortably and brushed cobwebs from his face and hands. He felt her sympathy, as once long, long ago, he had been aware of the sympathy of Billy Maughan. When she defended him, he learned more. His family were clearly in good hands, being treasured by someone called Daisy.

But when Albert came forward to look at him more closely, Soobie received a shock that made him want desperately to speak or move. It was Albert! *Albert Pond!* If I could talk, thought Soobie, what things I could say! If I could move and touch his hand, surely he would remember me. Albert looked at him, seeing only a blue rag doll and never suspecting that this doll had once been a dear friend of his.

By the time these visitors left the attic, Soobie knew that at least he would not be left in that one place to gather dust forever.

I will be taken to join my family, he thought, to sit

among them as if I were as dead as they. At that
thought, the bit of him that was still alive wept, and
wished profoundly for oblivion. It seemed to be a problem with only one solution.

Then, suddenly, months of patient suffering gave way
to anger. His heart cried out savagely to its maker, in-
sisting upon being heard.

"If I must live," it said, "and live and live, you
cannot leave me. You cannot leave *us!*

"If I must live," it said, "and live forever, so must
you.

"Either restore us all to life," it said, "or teach me
to die."

This was no self-pitying prayer. It was a howl of
indignation, as if some creature bound hand and foot
were rattling its chains. The whole house groaned, and
the sighing of it was heard within the halls of Heaven.

and go. She needed time to think. If the house in Elmtree Road were sold too quickly, she might be rushed into a move she could regret.

Lorna and Albert said little about the attic and nothing at all about the blue doll, except that there was another small job that needed doing. Jennifer changed the subject immediately, but did not look displeased. Albert, suspecting the truth, gave his mother-in-law a smile that was almost conspiratorial.

Somewhere upstairs, Ian and Keith could be heard having an argument. Anna was playing her recorder, the same set of notes, over and over again. When Matthew began to cry, Lorna decided it was time to go home. The house in Calder Park was so beautifully quiet.

All in all, it was an ordinary, unremarkable evening.

But in the attic at Number 5 Brocklehurst Grove, something was about to happen. *Something wonderful.*

Through the two grimy skylight windows, the evening sunlight filtered in onto the dust and the cobwebs. Perfect stillness, total silence. Then, oh then, the chair began to rock with a slow and gentle motion. And Soobie, as if suddenly awakened from a dream, sat up straight, and turned his wrist to look at his watch. It was seven-thirty P.M. on Saturday the tenth of May.

At Number 39 North Shore Road, at that precise moment, a more vigorous action broke the stillness. A purple foot kicked its way irascibly out of the counterpane.

Kate Penshaw was returning to her people. . . .

❧ 35 ❧

Saturday Evening

It was Saturday evening.

Billy Maughan had just managed to catch the three o'clock bus and was safely home at Bedemarsh Farm after his first outing to Castledean all on his own. He was still mystified about the dolls, but happy at having accomplished the journey. It made him feel like "a proper-sized" person!

"No problems?" said Molly.

"None at all," said Billy, "Aunt Daisy sends her love, and she says I can go and see her any time."

Daisy had shut up the shop on North Shore Road and had been ferried home in her taxi. She didn't even go upstairs to see the Mennyms—once a day was enough for that staircase. The time she'd gone up and down twice, first with the Ponds and then with Jamie's family, had left her feeling shattered all next day. Her little bungalow in Hartside Gardens might lack character, but it was a more practical place to live.

In Elmtree Road, the Gladstones had been discussing the latest prospective buyer for their home, a young couple who seemed quite keen, but had other properties to look it. Jennifer, still undecided about Brocklehurst Grove, was quite content to let the "buyer's" come . . .